SUGAR CREEK GANG
THE GREEN TENT MYSTERY

SUGAR CREEK GANG

THE GREEN TENT MYSTERY

Original title:
Green Tent Mystery at Sugar Creek

Paul Hutchens

MOODY PRESS • CHICAGO

The Green Tent Mystery at Sugar Creek

Copyright 1950 by
Paul Hutchens

Moody Press Edition 1969

ISBN 0-8024-4819-4

15 16 Printing/LC/Year 93 92 91

Printed in the United States of America

1

IT WAS THE DARKEST SUMMER NIGHT I ever saw—the night we accidentally stumbled onto a brand new mystery at Sugar Creek.

Imagine coming happily home with two of your best pals, carrying a string of seven fish, and feeling wonderful and proud. And then, halfway home, when you are passing an old, abandoned cemetery, imagine seeing a light out there and somebody digging! All of a sudden you get a creeping sensation in your spine and your red hair under your straw hat starts to try to stand up!

Well, that's the way it started. Nobody from Sugar Creek had been buried in that old cemetery for years and years, and it was only good for wild strawberries to grow in and bumblebees to make their nests in and barefoot boys to have their gang meetings in, telling ghost stories to each other.

And yet there it was, as plain as the crooked nose on Dragonfly's thin face, or the short, wide nose on Poetry's fat face, or the freckled nose on mine—an honest-to-goodness man or something, digging in the light of a kerosene lantern. The lantern itself was standing beside the tall tombstone of Sarah Paddler, Old Man Paddler's dead wife, and was shedding a spooky light on the man and his nervous movements as he scooped the yellowish-brown dirt out of the hole and piled it onto a fast-growing pile beside him.

I knew he couldn't see us because we were crouched behind some elder bushes that grew along the rail fence just outside the cemetery, but I also knew that if we made the slightest noise he might hear us; and if he heard us—well, what would he do?

I kept hoping Dragonfly's nose, which as everybody knows is almost always allergic to almost everything, wouldn't smell something that would make him sneeze, because Dragonfly had the craziest sneeze of anybody in the world—like a small squeal with a whistling tail on it. If Dragonfly would sneeze, it would be like the story every child should know, of Peter Rabbit running away from Mr. McGregor. As you may remember, Peter Rabbit was running lickety-sizzle, trying to get away from Mr. McGregor, the gardener. Spying a large sprinkling can, Peter jumped into it to hide himself. The can happened to have water in the bottom and that was too bad for poor Peter Rabbit's nose. Right away Peter sneezed and Mr. McGregor heard it, and Peter had to jump his wet-footed, wet-furred self out of the can and go racing furiously in some direction or other to get away from mad Mr. McGregor and his garden rake.

"Listen," Poetry hissed beside me.

I listened but couldn't hear a thing except the scooping sounds the shovel was making.

Then Poetry, who had his hand on my arm, squeezed my arm so tight I almost said "Ouch" just as I heard a new sound like the shovel had struck something hard.

"He's struck a rock," I said.

"Rock nothing," Poetry answered. "I'd know that sound anywhere. That was metal scraping on metal or maybe somebody's old coffin."

Poetry's nearly always-squawking voice broke when he said that and he sounded like a frog with laryngitis.

As you know, Dragonfly was the only one of us who was a little more afraid of a cemetery than the rest. So when Poetry said that like that, Dragonfly said, "Let's get out of here! Let's go home!"

Well, I had read different stories in my life about buried treasure. In fact, our own gang had stumbled onto a buried treasure mystery when we were on a camping trip up North and which you can read about in some of the other Sugar Creek Gang books. So when I was peeking through the foliage of the elder bush and between the rails of that tumbledown old rail fence, watching the strange things in a graveyard at a strange hour of the night, say! I was all of a sudden all set to get myself tangled up in another mystery just as quick as I could—that is, if I could without getting into too much danger at the same time, for, as

7

Dad says, "It is better to have good sense and try to use it than it is to be brave."

Just that second I heard a bobwhite whistling, "Bob-white! Bob-white! Poor Bob-white!" It was a very cheery bird call—the kind I would almost rather hear around Sugar Creek than any other.

As fast as a firefly's fleeting flash, my mind's eye was seeing a ten-inch-long, burnished-brown-beaked bird with a white stomach and a white forehead. The feathers on the crown of its head were shaped like the topknot on a topknotted chicken.

The man kept on shoveling, not paying attention to anything except what he was doing. He seemed to be working faster though. Then all of a sudden he stopped while he was in a stooped-over position and for a jiffy didn't make a move.

"He's looking at something in the hole," Poetry whispered. "He sees something."

"Maybe he's listening," I said, which it seemed like he was—like a robin does on our front lawn with its head cocked to one side, waiting to see or hear—or both—a night crawler push part of itself out of its hole. Then she makes a headfirst dive for the worm, holds on for dear life while she yanks and pulls till she gets its slimy body out. Then she eats it or else pecks it to death and into small pieces and flies with it to her nest to feed it to her babies.

A jiffy later I heard another birdcall and it was another whistling sound—a very mournful cry that sounded like, "Coo-oo, coo-oo, coo-oo"—and it was a turtledove.

Say! It was just as though that sad, plaintive turtledove call had scared the living daylights out of the man. He straightened up, looked all around and came to quick life, picked up the lantern and started walking toward the old maple tree on the opposite side of the cemetery.

"He's got a limp," Poetry said. "Look how he drags one foot after him."

I didn't have time to wrack my brain to see if I could remember if I knew anybody who had that kind of limp because no sooner had the man reached the maple tree than he lifted the lantern up to his face and blew out the light. Then I heard a car door slam, the sound of a motor starting; and then two headlights lit up the whole cemetery for a second, and two long, blinding beams made a wide sweep across the top of Strawberry Hill, lit up the tombstones and the lonely old pine tree above Sarah Paddler's grave and the chokecherry shrubs and even the elder bush we were hiding behind. Then the car went racing down the abandoned lane that led to the road not more than three blocks away, leaving us three boys wondering "What on earth?" and "Why?" and "Who?" and "Where?"

It seemed like I couldn't move—I had been crouched in such a cramped position for so long a time.

It was Dragonfly who thought of something that

added to the mystery when he said, "First time I ever heard a bobwhite whistling in the night like that."

The very second he said it I wished I had thought of it first; but I did think of something else first. Anyway I *said* it first—and it was, "Yeah, and whoever heard of a turtledove cooing in the night?"

"It's just plain cuckoo," Poetry said. "I'll bet there was somebody over there in that car waiting for him and maybe watching and those whistles meant something special. They probably meant 'Danger! Look out! Get away, quick!'"

Then Poetry said in an authoritative voice like he was the leader of our gang instead of Big Jim who is when he is with us—and I am when Big Jim isn't— "Let's go take a look at what he was doing."

"Let's go home," Dragonfly said.

"Why, Dragonfly *Gilbert!*" I said. "Go on home yourself if you are scared! Poetry and I have got to investigate!"

"I'm not sc-scared," Dragonfly said—and was.

As quick as we were sure the car was really gone, I turned on my dad's big, long, three-batteried flashlight—I having had it with me—and Poetry, Dragonfly and I started to climb through the rail fence to go toward the mound of yellowish-brown earth beside Sarah Paddler's tombstone.

2

As I SAID, the three of us started to climb through the rail fence to go to the hole in the ground and investigate what had been going on there. It took us only a jiffy or two to get through the fence—Poetry squeezing his fat self through first, since he is almost twice as big around as either Dragonfly or I. If he could get through, we knew we could too.

I carried the flashlight, Dragonfly the string of seven fish, and Poetry carried himself. To get to the mound of earth we had to wind our way around, among chokecherry shrubs, wild rosebushes with reddish roses on them, mullein stalks and different kinds of wild flowers, such as blue vervain, and especially ground ivy, which I noticed had a lot of dark purple flowers on it—the same color as the vervain. The ground ivy flower clusters were scattered among the notched heart-shaped leaves of the vine.

In a jiffy we were there and the three of us were standing around the hole in the form of a right-angle triangle. An imaginary line running from Poetry to me made the hypotenuse of the right-angle triangle, I thought, and another imaginary line running from Dragonfly to me would make the base of the triangle.

There wasn't a thing to see in the hole except a lot of fresh dirt. In fact, there wasn't a thing of any interest whatever to a guy like Poetry who was the kind of boy that was always looking for a clue of some kind —and especially a mystery—to jump out at him like a jack-in-the-box does in a toy store when you press a spring.

The only thing that happened, while we were standing half-scared in that silence, looking down into the hole and at the mound of yellowish-brown earth, was that, all of a sudden, a big beetle came zooming out of the darkness and landed with a whamety-sizzle-kerplop against the side of my freckled face, bounced off and landed upside down on the top of the yellowish-brown earth where it began wriggling and twisting and trying to get off its back and onto its six spiny-looking legs.

Anybody who knows anything about bugs and beetles knows that a June bug isn't a bug but is a beetle, and has two different names, one of them being a June beetle and the other a May beetle, depending upon whichever month of the year it flies around in the country where you live.

I was searching every corner of my mind to see if I could imagine anything I was seeing was a clue to help us solve the new mystery which we had just discovered. Who in the world was the man and why had he been here? Why had he gotten scared when he heard the bobwhite and the turtledove?

I was remembering that June beetles get awful

hungry at night and they eat the foliage of oak and willow and poplar trees. In the daytime they hide themselves in the soil of anybody's pasture or in the grass in the woods. June beetles are crazy about lights at night, and the very minute they see one they make a beetle-line for it just like the one which right that second was struggling on its back on the mound of earth.

"Crazy old June beetle!" I said and Poetry answered, "June *what?*"

"Crazy old June *beetle,*" I said, shining my flashlight directly on it, and pushing the light up close to its brown ridiculous-looking body so that Poetry and Dragonfly could see what I was talking about.

Poetry in a disgusted voice said, "When are you going to get over that buggy idea of studying insects?"

I knew I might get over it almost anytime like I generally do some new hobby, which I pick up in the summer. But I didn't want anybody to make fun of the fun I was having studying insects. Dad and I were having more fun than you can shake a stick at, catching different kinds of insects that summer, especially beetles, which anybody knows have four wings. The two wings in front are not used for flying but are like a hard rainproof roof protecting its two *flying* wings, which, when the beetle isn't flying, are all nicely folded up underneath like two colored umbrellas.

Little Jim was always collecting things too and he was to blame for inspiring me to start a collection of my own. That summer Little Jim was looking up different kinds of wild flowers and writing their names down in a notebook. It just so happened that that week Dad and I were studying beetles and other insects.

Just that minute the big brown beetle I had my flashlight focused on, wriggled itself off the clod of dirt it was on and went tumblety-sizzle down on the side of the mound and landed kerplop in the grave itself.

"Poor little scarab beetle," I said to it. "I'll bet that right this very second one of your nearest relatives is in that great big yellow-stomached catfish I caught a half hour ago at the mouth of the branch."

Anybody knows that one of the best baits in the world to catch a catfish at night is a juicy grub worm, which is a little C-shaped larva which hatches out of an egg of a scarab beetle, such as a June beetle or some other kind.

"You'd be scared too," Poetry said, "if you were flying around at night and saw a light in a cemetery accidentally and all of a sudden found yourself right in the bottom of a newly dug grave."

"Poetry," I said. "I didn't say *scared*—I said *scarab*." Then, feeling kind of proud of all the different things Dad and I had learned that week, I began to rattle off some of it to Poetry: "That's what kind of beetle it is," I said, "only it doesn't eat dead stuff like some scarab beetles do. Its larvae eat the roots of nearly everything Dad plants in our new ground, but most scarabs eat dead things and worse stuff."

"Cut out the education!" Poetry said. "Who cares about that? I s'pose you think that's why he flew into this old cemetery in the first place. He was looking for something dead to eat. Maybe that's why he dived headfirst into the side of your face!"

"Cut it out, yourself," I said, feeling a little temper-fire starting in my mind.

Just then the June beetle unscrambled himself—or herself, whichever it was—spread its shell-like front wings and its reddish-brown back wings and took off again, straight in the direction of my face, but I snapped off the flashlight quick and ducked my head, and he missed me and disappeared into the night—on his way, maybe, to the lighted window of somebody's house. If he should happen to see one somewhere, and if there should be a window open without a screen, some woman or girl would soon be screaming bloody murder for a man or boy to come and save her life.

"Turn your light on again, quick!" Dragonfly said. "Let's get out of here!" He quickly started to do it himself, but we stopped him.

We looked all around everywhere but still couldn't find a single clue to tell why whoever he was had been digging there.

"Hey!" Poetry exclaimed excitedly all of a sudden. "Look! Here's a clear shoe print in the soft dirt."

Then like he had seen a ghost or something, he almost screamed as he said, "It's a *woman's* high-heeled shoe!"

"What on earth!" I thought.

"But it was a m-m-m-*man* digging!" Dragonfly said, stammering.

"Then it was a woman dressed in overalls!" I said in the most excited voice I had ever heard myself use in a long time.

I stooped, shoved Dad's powerful three-batteried flashlight down into the neat little shoe print. "Say, she had very small feet," I said.

Naturally, there wasn't anything extramysterious about a woman wearing overalls around Sugar Creek, especially when she was doing the kind of hard work which men have to do and which some women have to do sometimes. But what would a woman be doing digging in an abandoned cemetery late at night?

"What on earth?" I said.

Not a one of us knew what to do or say next so we decided to go over to the old maple tree. The minute we got there Poetry ordered me to shine my light around the tree trunk while he studied the bark to see if any of it had been freshly knocked off.

"What are you looking for?" I asked.

"To see if a *human* bobwhite or a *human* turtledove was hiding up there among the branches as a sort of lookout for the woman. Those two bird whistles were warnings of some kind."

16

What Poetry said made sense, but we couldn't stay all night, and our six parents would be wondering why we didn't come home—and also worrying. Any boy who has good sense doesn't like to do any dumb thing to make his parents worry any more than they would do anyway, because a parent is something a boy would have a hard time doing without especially when it is time for breakfast or dinner or supper. Besides, who would give him a licking when he needed it, which every once in a while he probably does, even if he's just had one the week before?

So we decided to go on home, get secret word to the rest of the gang—Big Jim, Circus, Little Jim and Little Tom Till—to all meet us at the old pine tree beside Sarah Paddler's tombstone tomorrow right after lunch. Then we could look to see if we could find out what had been going on: why a limping woman in overalls was digging in an old abandoned cemetery, and who had given the bobwhite and turtledove calls and why.

"Let's go home and get some sleep," I said to Dragonfly and Poetry, and we started up the lane to the highway following an old brown path, which twenty minutes ago the car had followed.

Then what to my wondering ears should come, from back in the direction of the open grave and Sarah Paddler's tombstone but a quail's sharp, clear call. "Bob-white! Bob-white! Poor Bob-white."

Say, Dragonfly, who had been standing there under the tree with us, his teeth chattering, jumped like a

17

firecracker had exploded under him, whirled into fast life, and a jiffy later his spindly legs were flying like a June beetle's wings, carrying him up the lane toward the road that would lead us home.

As fast as two other firecrackers getting exploded from the explosion of the first one, Poetry and I were dashing madly after Dragonfly, I getting more scared the faster I ran. We didn't stop until, panting and gasping for breath, we got to my house.

Say, the very second we came panting into our yard and up to the iron pitcher pump at the end of the boardwalk about twenty feet from our back door, Dad came sauntering up from the direction of the barn, carrying a kerosene lantern and—would you believe it?—*a spade and a shovel!*

"Wh-what are you doing, still up?" I said, still panting and a little mixed up in my mind.

"Oh, just digging around in the earth a little," Dad said in a lazy, yawning voice. "Been burying something or other."

Say, three boys looked at each other from three different directions and felt terribly disappointed, for it looked like our mystery was going to explode right in front of our worried faces.

"Somebody die?" Poetry asked, trying to be mischievous at a time when he shouldn't have.

Dad said indifferently, "Just a couple of newborn pigs. Old Red Addie gave us a new family of eight tonight. Two of them didn't live so I thought I'd bury 'em right away."

After being half-scared to death, here our mystery was all solved, I thought—or was it? How about the woman's shoe tracks and the mysterious birdcalls and the car?

Well, we divided our seven fish into three equal parts. Poetry took three sunfish, Dragonfly three and I took the big catfish, which I myself had caught on the descendant—or else what might have become the ancestor—of a June beetle. That big, yellow-stomached catfish was as big as three sunfish—in fact, as big as all six of the insignificant fish which Dragonfly and Poetry had pulled in after the fish had accidentally hooked themselves onto their merely worm-baited hooks and gotten themselves pulled in to shore.

3

NEXT DAY we managed to get the news around quick to all the rest of the gang—but secretly because it seemed like our parents ought not to know what was going on until we ourselves investigated. Anybody knows a mystery isn't a mystery any longer if someone explains it, and there's nobody that can spoil a boy's mystery any quicker than his very bright parents who always know almost everything anyway—one reason being that our dads used to be boys themselves.

The very second I finished all of my dinner that day —except my piece of apple pie—I looked past Dad's overhanging, reddish-brown eyebrows to where Mom sat at the end of the table. "May I be excused and eat my pie outdoors?" I asked.

You see, if there is anything I would rather do than anything else, it is to leave the table early, before anybody thinks about starting to do the dishes, and take my three-cornered, one-sixth of an apple pie, and go out our east screen door with the pie in one hand and my straw hat in the other, swing out to our grape arbor, step up on a strong, wooden box, which is always there, reach up and lay the pie on top of the two-by-four crossbeam at the east end of the arbor where there isn't any vine growing. Then I like to climb up and sit on the top with the cool breeze blowing in my freckled face and my two bare feet with their ten stubby toes swinging below me. I hold the nicely crusted pie upside down and eat it that way, while I look around the Sugar Creek territory to where different members of our gang live. I also like to look at our farm and the barn and the chicken house and the big walnut tree with the long rope swing hanging from the first branch, which grows on the south side, and the plum tree with the robin's nest in the three-limbed crotch up near the top. Boy, oh boy, does it make me feel fine and glad to be alive, especially glad to be a boy!

Even while I was asking to be excused, I was imagining myself already outdoors, sitting up on the flat side of the two-by-four crossbeam.

But say, Dad was as smart as I was—smart enough to read my mind—and he saw things in it that I hardly knew were there. Because right that second he looked at Mom and said, "There are some good habits, some bad habits, and some that are in between. The ones in between don't hurt a boy very much, but they help to make him *him*.

"That's getting to be quite a habit with you, Bill," he finished, looking at me with his gray-green eyes.

I had been looking at the pie, which I already had in my hand, expecting Mom to say "Yes," like she nearly always does.

"What habit?" I said innocently to Dad.

"Use plain American, Theodore," Mom said to Dad. "The boy doesn't understand philosophy."

And Dad said to Mom with a mischievous twinkle in his eye, "May I take my pie and go outdoors and eat it upside down on top of our grape arbor?"

Mom looked up at him with a sort of quizzical expression on her face. There was also a twinkle in her eye that seemed funny to Dad, but not to me. Then she said, "Certainly. You can do that while Bill and I do the dishes."

Dad said, "Thank you," and took his one-sixth of a pie in his big, hard, sun-tanned farmer hand, slipped out of his chair and outdoors fast, letting the screen slam hard behind him like I sometimes do—and shouldn't. Outside he let out a bloodcurdling war whoop and I heard his footsteps running toward the grape arbor.

A second later I was outdoors too.

Say, if there is anything that looks ridiculous, it is a boy's long-legged, red-haired, bushy-eyebrowed father grunting himself into an upside-down knot and out of it again while he climbs up onto a high grape arbor.

A jiffy later there was Dad up there where I should have been, with his heavy work shoes on his large feet swinging, and eating his pie upside down and panting for breath from all the unnecessary exercise. It was funny to Dad, but to me it looked silly; so I sat down

22

on the porch with my back to him and ate my pie right side up and for some reason it didn't taste very good.

It was a scorching hot day and I began to feel a little better there in the shade, when all of a sudden Mom said from inside the house, using a very cheerful voice, "OK, Bill. The dishes are all ready for you."

I always know when Mom calls me cheerfully like that she's trying to make me *want* to come.

But say, Dad turned out to be a really swell dad after all, or else he was trying to give me a free education. It seemed like he was still pretending to be me up there on that grape arbor so when he heard Mom say "dishes," he called out cheerfully, "Coming," and swung around quick and down off the grape arbor and hurried into the house like he would rather dry the Collins family dinner dishes than do anything else in the whole world.

He got stopped at the door by Mom though, who was maybe trying to play the game with him, and she said, "Wipe that dirt off your shoes on the mat there" —which she tells me about thirty-seven times a day— sometimes even while I am already doing it, having thought of it first myself. Say, I looked at Dad's feet and they did have dirt on them—*a yellowish-brown dirt on the sides of the soles and heels!*

At the very second I saw Dad's shoes with yellowish-brown dirt on them instead of the very black dirt I knew was the kind that was under the pignut trees, I wondered what on *earth?* I certainly didn't want my dad to be really getting mixed up in our mystery like I had thought last night for a minute he might be.

Not only that—I didn't want him to have been the person who had given the bobwhite and turtledove birdcalls last night, which my discouraged mind was trying to tell me he could have been.

Not knowing I was going to say what I did, I said, "Dad!" in a loud and astonished voice. *"Where* did you get that kind of mud on your shoes?" I was using the kind of voice I had heard another member of our family use on me several different times in my life.

Dad, who was already wiping off his shoes on the mat at the door, looked down at them in astonishment and said, "What dirt?"

Mom's astonished voice shot through the finely woven screen. "Why, Theodore Collins! What on *earth?"*

Dad grinned back through the screen at her and said, "No, not *what on earth,* but *earth on what?"* which I could tell he thought was funny, but Mom didn't think it was very. She went on in her same astonished, accusing voice, saying, "Those are the very same muddy shoes you ate dinner with!"

"I never ate dinner with muddy shoes in my life," Dad said, with a grin in his voice. "I always use a knife and fork and spoon," which was supposed to be extra funny—and was to Dad and me—but for some reason Mom only smiled rather than laughed and it looked like she was trying to keep herself from even smiling.

"Go get your father's house slippers," Mom ordered me, and I obeyed her in a tickled hurry.

Dad slipped his feet out of his shoes and left them on the porch, and slipped his feet into his slippers and ordered me to follow him into the house, which I also did with a little less speed, because I could tell by the tone of his voice that he had some work for me to do, which I found out was the truth.

It wasn't too bad though 'cause Dad and I played a little game while we did the dishes. He called me "Dad" and I called him "Bill." He ordered Mom to go into the front room to look after my baby sister, Charlotte Ann.

Say, Dad and I dived headfirst—or rather, I should say *hands* first—into the sudsy dishwater, making short work of those dishes, getting them done a lot faster than if a mother and daughter had done them. Also we hurried to be sure to get through before Mom might come out into the kitchen and look over our work and decide we were not using the right kind of soap or something.

It really was fun 'cause I kept giving orders to my red-haired, awkward son, giving him cuckoo commands every few minutes, such as "Keep your mind on your work, Bill!" "Hey, that plate has to be wiped over again!" "Your mother likes to have the glasses polished a little better than that, son. We never know.

when there might be company from somewhere and those glasses have to shine like everything"—unnecessary things a father nearly always says to a boy.

Well, those dishes got done in about half the usual time. As quick as they were finished, I was free to start to do what I really wanted to do in just the way I wanted to do it, but I got stopped by Dad's big, gruff voice. I had just tossed Dad's drying towel toward the rack beside the stove, and missed the rack and had made a red-headfirst dive for it to pick it up quick before Dad, or especially Mom, might see it. I was still in a bent-over position—just right for a good spank from somebody—when Dad's voice socked me and the words were, "Which one of us is Bill and which is your father now—for the rest of the afternoon, I mean?"

"I am," I said. In half a jiffy the towel was on the rack nice and straight and I was over by the washstand, stooping to get my straw hat, which was beside Dad's big work shoes.

"Bring the gang home sometime this afternoon," Dad said. "I want to show them Addie's nice, new red-haired family."

"I will," I answered, having seen the six cute little quadrupeds myself that morning.

By that time I was already outdoors and ten feet from the slammed screen door, the door having slammed itself because of a strong, coiled spring. Then Dad called again and stopped me stock-still. "If

26

I am your father again, and you are Bill Collins, you had better stay home and mow the lawn and let me go to meet the gang"—but I could tell he didn't mean it. Dad looked awfully cute, I thought, with Mom's big apron on and his blue shirt sleeves rolled up to the elbows, his slippers still on, standing in the open screen door.

I called to him saying, "I am still Theodore Collins and you are Bill and you are letting flies in. Shut the door quick—and *quietly!*"

As I hurried away, my mischievous dad called after me, "So long, Mr. Collins! Have a nice time, and don't forget to find a new beetle for our collection."

"So long, Bill!" I yelled from the front gate, which I had just opened and gone through and shut after me. Then as I dashed past "Theodore Collins" on our mailbox I was myself again. I swished across the dusty road, vaulted over the old lichen-covered rail fence and in a jiffy was running in the path that had been made by barefoot boys, down through the woods as fast as I could go to the spring where the gang was going to meet first before going up to the top of Strawberry Hill to the cemetery.

4

Boy, oh boy! I never felt better in my life than I did when I was galloping through that woods to meet the gang. First I was in the sunlight and then in the shade as I raced along on that winding little brown path—swishing past different kinds of trees, such as maple, beech, ash, oak and also dodging around chokecherry shrubs and wild rosebushes with roses scattered all around among the thorns, also past dogwood trees and all kinds of wild flowers that grew on either side of the path.

Even though I had had to be delayed unnecessarily because of the dishes, I got to the spring about the same time Little Jim and Poetry did. Circus was already there in the favorite place where he usually waits for us when he gets there first, which is in the top branches of a little elm sapling that grows at the top of the steep bank. As you know, at the bottom of that steep bank is the spring itself, but we always meet in a little shaded, open space at the top. Circus was swinging and swaying and looked really like a chimpanzee, hanging by his hands and feet and everything except his tail—which he didn't have anyway.

As quick as Big Jim, with his almost moustache, and Little Tom Till, with his freckled face and red hair, and Dragonfly, with his goggle-eyed face and spindling legs got there, that was all of us.

Poetry, Dragonfly and I told everybody everything that had happened last night, but I didn't tell them about Dad having had yellowish-brown dirt on his shoes, and with my eyes I kept Poetry and Dragonfly from telling them about the two baby pigs Dad had buried somewhere, because I felt sure Dad wouldn't bury two baby pigs in a cemetery which had been reserved for human beings only.

A little later, after a loafing ramble along the bayou and a climb to the top of Strawberry Hill, we scrambled over the rail fence and in a couple of jiffies reached the place where the woman had been digging last night, which was not more than ten feet from Sarah Paddler's tall tombstone. Well, we all stopped and stood around in a barefoot circle looking down into the hole. Sure enough—just as we had seen it last night—there was the print of a high-heeled shoe and also other high-heeled shoe tracks all around, but none of the others were as clear as the one we were all studying that very minute.

"What on earth do you s'pose she was digging here for?" Little Tom Till asked in his high-pitched voice.

Big Jim answered him saying, "If we knew that, we would know what we want to know."

For a minute I focused my eyes on the hand which

somebody had chiseled on Sarah Paddler's tombstone. One finger of the hand pointed toward the sky. I had read the words just below the hand maybe a hundred and twenty times in my life and they were: "There is rest in heaven," which I knew there was for anybody who got to go there. When I was in a cemetery, it was easy to think about things like that. I was sort of dreamily remembering that our minister in the Sugar Creek church says that there is only one way for a boy to get to heaven. First, the boy has to believe that he is an honest-to-goodness sinner and needs a Saviour. Then he has to believe that Jesus, who is the Saviour, came all the way from heaven a long time ago to die for him and to save him from his sins; then if the boy will open the door of his heart and let the Saviour come in, that will settle it.

Our minister, who knows many verses in the Bible by heart, tells the people that come to our church that there isn't any other way for anybody to be saved except just like I told you.

So I knew that Old Man Paddler, who was saved himself and was the kindest long-whiskered old man that ever was a friend to a boy, would see his wife Sarah again—maybe the very minute he got to heaven.

For a fast jiffy, while I was standing by the hole which the June beetle had tumbled into last night and was looking up at that carved hand on the tombstone, my mind sort of drifted away on a friendly little journey clear up into heaven—past the great big white cumulus cloud that was piling itself up in the south-west right that minute above the tree-covered hills where I knew Old Man Paddler's cabin was. I imagined that somewhere in heaven maybe there was a very nice little cabin waiting for that kind old man, and that his wife Sarah was out there in the garden somewhere looking after the flowers for him. Every now and then she would stop doing what she was doing and look toward a little white gate like the one we have at our house by the big swing near the walnut tree to see if she could see her husband coming. Then all of a sudden I imagined she did see him and her kind, oldish face lit up like Mom's does sometimes when she sees Dad coming home from somewhere, and she started quick on a half walk and half run out across the yard to meet him, calling, "Hi there! I've been waiting for you a long time."

It was a terribly nice thought. Only I knew that if that old man ever left Sugar Creek, it would be awful lonesome around here for a long time, and it sort of seemed like we needed him here even worse than his wife did up there.

*   *   *

From Sarah Paddler's grave in the shade of the big pine tree, we went all the way across the cemetery, winding around a little to get to the old maple where last night I had shone my flashlight all around looking for signs of a human quail or a human turtledove.

There we stopped in the friendly shade and lay

down in the tall grass to hold a meeting to help us decide what to do next. While we were lying there in seven different directions, chewing the juicy ends of bluegrass and timothy and wild rye, Big Jim gave a special order which was, "I would like each of us except Poetry and Dragonfly to give a quail whistle."

"Why?" Little Tom Till wanted to know.

"I want to find out if any of you were out here last night making those calls. I also want to know if any of you guys were out here dressed in overalls and wearing a woman's high-heeled shoes."

Little Jim and Little Tom Till and Circus and Big Jim himself did the best they could making bobwhite calls and Circus was the only one of us whose whistle sounded like the quail whistle we had heard last night.

Then Big Jim made all of us, except Poetry, Dragonfly and me, do a turtledove call; and again Circus was the only one whose call was like the one we heard last night.

"OK, Circus." Big Jim leveled his eyes across our little tangled-up circle and said to him, "Confess or we will drag you down to Sugar Creek and throw you in."

"All right," Circus said, "I confess I was home in bed sound asleep when I heard those calls last night."

"So was I," Little Tom Till said.

"So was I," Little Jim echoed.

"Yeah, and so was I. Sound asleep in bed listening to the calls," Big Jim said sarcastically.

Well, that left only Poetry, Dragonfly and me, and we were the ones who had heard the calls in the first place, so the mystery was still unsolved as it had been, not a one of us believing that Circus was there last night.

There wasn't any use to stay where we were, so, it being a very hot afternoon, we decided to go to the old swimming hole and get cooled off.

"Last one in is a bear's tail," Circus yelled back at us over one of his square shoulders as he galloped off first, out across the cemetery to the other side.

The rest of us quick took off after him, not a one of us wanting to be a bear's tail, which means we would have to be almost nothing because bears have very stubby tails.

Long before we got there nearly everyone of us had his shirt off—so that by the time we should get there all we would have to do would be to wrestle ourselves out of our overalls and in a jiffy we would be out in the middle of the swellest water to swim in in the whole world. Everyone of us knew how to swim like a fish, for our parents had made us learn as soon as we were old enough to—like everybody in the world should.

Say, you should have seen the way our mystery began to come to life while we were still on the shore before splashing ourselves in.

All of a sudden Little Jim, who was undressing in the shade of a willow where he always hangs his clothes, yelled to us in a very excited voice for him, "Hey, Bill! Circus! Poetry! Everybody! Come here quick! Hurry! Look what I found!"

Well, when Little Jim or any of our gang calls in an excited voice like that, it always sends a half-dozen thrills through me because it nearly always means something extraspecial.

Before I knew it, I was galloping across to where he was, my shirt in one hand and one of my overall legs in the other, getting there as quick as the rest of us. I also managed to grab up a stick on my way just in case Little Jim might have spied a water moccasin or some other kind of snake, of which there are maybe twenty different varieties around Sugar Creek.

Little Jim was standing there holding his clothes in one hand and pointing down with an excited right forefinger to something on the ground on a little strip of sand at the water's edge.

At first I didn't see a thing, except some shaded water where about fifty or more small, black, flat whirligig beetles were racing around in excited circles on the surface of the water. Right away I smelled ripe apples, which is the kind of odor a whirligig beetle gives off. Anybody who knows anything about whirligig beetles knows that smell comes from a kind of milky fluid which they use to protect themselves from being eaten by fish or some kind of water bird or something else.

Even Poetry didn't see what Little Jim was excited about. "Education again," he said with a disgruntled snort and turned back to the swimming hole.

Dragonfly, who wasn't interested in Dad's and my new hobby, grunted too and also sneezed, saying, "I'm allergic to the smell of *sweet bugs*"—that being a common name for those lively little ripe-apple-smelling beetles.

"They're whirligig beetles," I said, wanting to defend Little Jim for calling us over in such an excited voice for what the rest of the gang would think was almost nothing.

"Look, everybody! Look! See, it's a clue!" Little Jim yelled.

Then my eyes dived in the direction his finger was really pointing and I saw what he saw. Boy, oh boy! A lively thrill started whirligigging in my very surprised brain, for what to my wondering eyes had appeared but, half hidden in the grass, a pair of women's new shoes—very small, expensive-looking white pumps with extrahigh heels and with a heart-shaped design across the toes that looked kind of like the leaves from a ground ivy, like the ones that grew all around Sarah Paddler's tombstone.

What on *earth*, I thought and remembered that Dad had said, "Earth on *what*?" when I saw there actually were some yellowish-brown earth stains on those extrahigh heels of those newish-looking, pretty women's shoes.

Just that second Dragonfly said, "Psst! Listen, everybody!"—which everybody did, and there it was again as plain as a Sugar Creek cloudless day, a sharp bobwhite call from down the creek somewhere: "Bobwhite! Bob-white! Poor-Bob-white!"

5

SAY, if that bobwhite call was from a real quail, then we didn't have anything to worry about. But we knew that honest-to-goodness quails not only don't make their very pretty calls in the middle of the night, but also they don't do it in the middle of a sultry, sunny midsummer afternoon—or if they do I don't remember having heard any do it around Sugar Creek.

If it was a human being calling like a quail, then what?

And if it was a *man* human being, we would all want to scramble ourselves out of there and hide somewhere so that whoever he was wouldn't see us. But if it was a *woman* human being who had made the quail call—which it might have been, I thought, because the woman's shoes were lying there in the sand beside Little Jim—then every single one of us ought to make a headfirst dive toward getting his clothes on.

Before we could start to try to decide what to do, we heard the quail call again and this time it was a lot nearer than it had been—in fact it seemed like it wasn't a hundred feet distant and had come from the direction of the spring from which we ourselves had just come. That meant that the person, man or woman, was maybe walking in the same path we had been running in a little while before. We wouldn't have even half enough time to get our clothes on before running to hide.

I looked all around our tense circle to see if the rest of the gang had any ideas as to what to do and it seemed like not a one of us could do a thing except stand stock-still, with his eyes and ears glued to the direction from which the last quail call had come.

"Quick, Dragonfly!" I heard myself say, taking charge of things. "Get those shoes, quick, and let's get out of here!" I shouldn't have tried to because Big Jim is our leader when he is with us.

Big Jim took my leadership away from me in a split second by saying, "Leave those shoes alone! Don't you dare touch them! If anything has happened, we don't want our fingerprints on them!"

In less than a fourth of a jiffy we were scrambling up the side of the slope leaving those shoes about eighteen inches from the whirligig beetles, and with all our minds whirligigging like everything—some of us with our clothes half on and others with them half off and the rest of the gang with them all off. We were getting ourselves out of there fast.

At the top of the little slope we came to the narrow footpath, zipped across it and disappeared into the tall corn—that being one of Dragonfly's dad's cornfields.

I knew that on the opposite side of that rather narrow strip of cornfield was the bayou, which was divided into two parts with a longish pond on either end of it, and each of those ponds had in it some very lazy water in which there were a few lone-wolf, mud pickerel, or barred pickerel, as some people call them. Between the two ponds there was a narrow strip of soggy, marshy soil and a little path that was bordered by giant ragweeds. This was a sort of shortcut to the woods from the old swimming hole. Once we got to the woods we could follow the rail fence like we had done last night and come out at the place where Little Jim had killed the bear, which you have probably read about in one of the other Sugar Creek Gang stories. As you know, that was at the bottom of Strawberry Hill; and at the top of the hill is the old cemetery and the hole in the ground beside Sarah Paddler's tombstone.

There we would be safe from whoever was coming up that path, nearer and nearer every second—that is, if he was dangerous.

As quick as we were far enough into the tall corn to be hidden from sight of the path, we dropped down on the ground to listen and to look to see if we could see what was going on. As you know, corn blades are not as thick at the bottom of the stalks as they are at the top so if anybody was coming up the path, we could see his feet if we were lying on the ground.

Poetry, who was real close to me like he nearly always is, whispered in my ear, "Hey, shh! There he is!"

I looked and saw the cuffs of somebody's trousers standing at the end of my corn row in the very place where we always left the path to dive down the incline into our willow-protected outdoor dressing room. Then came a startling quail call again and this time it seemed so near it almost scared me out of what few wits I hadn't already been scared out of.

I waited, wondering if there would be an answer, and then what to my astonished ears should come but the sound of a turtledove's low, sad, lonesome call from the other direction farther up the path.

Almost right away I saw the skirt of a woman's yellowish dress coming out of our green dressing room. I also noticed that she was barefoot. Straining my ears in their direction I could hear her talking and complaining about something like a boy does when he gets called by his mother to leave his play. I could hear the man's voice too, but I couldn't make out what he was saying.

A jiffy later I heard her say, "I was having so much fun wading in the riffles. Look! I found this—a big washboard shell! I'll bet I'll find a pearl in it! Wouldn't it be wonderful if I did find one worth hundreds of dollars?"

And I heard the man say, "That's fine, but it's time for your rest. Let's get back to the tent."

So! They were camping somewhere up in Old

Man Paddler's woods and that meant they would either have to get their drinking water at the spring where our gang met every day when our parents would let us, or they would have to come to our house to get it out of the iron pitcher pump at the end of the boardwalk twenty feet from our back door and not more than fifteen feet from our grape arbor.

For some reason it didn't make me feel very good. Of course, Old Man Paddler owned nearly all the territory around Sugar Creek and he had a right to let anybody camp on it that wanted to, but it seemed like the whole territory belonged to the gang, especially the woods around the spring because our bare feet had walked on nearly every square inch of it. We had climbed nearly every tree and rested in the shade of every one of them and it was too much like having company at our house. You don't feel free to yell and scream and give loon calls and go screeching through the woods, yelling like wild Indians or anything, when somebody strange is camping there. You even have to comb your hair when you are outdoors if there happens to be a city woman around.

I thought and felt all that while we were still lying on the sandy soil of Dragonfly's dad's cornfield and the man and the woman were still not more than a few rods up the path on their way toward the spring.

They were out of hearing distance now, but I could see the movement the tall weeds were making as they swayed back into place after the man and woman had gone through, and the movement was like it is when the wind blows across our wheat field.

A jiffy later they were gone and I could hear only the sound of the breathing of seven half-dressed, half-undressed boys.

"What on *earth*?" I said using my nervous voice before any of the rest of the gang did.

Circus, trying to be funny, said, "Seven boys are."

We would have to go in swimming now to get the sand of Dragonfly's cornfield off ourselves. Besides I had some dirt in my red hair too and it would have to be dived out.

It was a not-very-happy gang of boys that sneaked back to our green, leaf-shaded dressing room and went in swimming.

"Did any of you guys hear him say 'Let's get back to the tent'?" I asked.

"Sure," Poetry said, "what of it?"

"What of it?" I exclaimed. "Why, that means they are camping up there in the woods somewhere, and we'll have to be scared half to death every time we go in swimming for fear some woman and her husband will hear or see us, or else we'll have to wear bathing suits." None of our gang had ever worn one in our whole lives.

I had just come up from diving and was shaking the water out of my ears and rubbing it out of my eyes so I could hear and see, when our mystery came to livelier life than before.

It happened like this. Little Jim had already finished swimming and was dressing over by the willow where he always dresses and where the whirligig beetles were still in swimming having a sweet time going round and round on the surface of the water like boys and girls skating on Sugar Creek in the wintertime.

Little Jim had just finished shoving his head through the neck of his shirt and was reaching for his overalls that were hanging on the willow when all of a sudden he let out another excited yell like he had done before. "Hey, Bill! Circus! Poetry! Everybody! Come here quick! Hurry! Look what I found. It's somebody's billfold!"

By the time I got the water out of my ears and eyes and could see, I saw him holding up a pretty brown billfold like the kind Mom carries in her handbag.

Not waiting to finish getting the water out of my ears and eyes, I went splashety-gallop straight for Little Jim, who was on the shore by the willow still holding up the brown leather billfold for us to see. Nearly all the rest of the gang were already splashing their different ways toward Little Jim and almost all of us got there at the same time.

Say, when those black, flat, oval whirligig beetles saw or heard or felt us coming out of our swimming hole toward theirs, they got scared. In a jiffy, like whirligig beetles do when they are badly frightened, they stopped going around in their fast, excited circles and dived under the water to hide themselves on the bottom of Sugar Creek so that by the time I got there, there wasn't one in sight and only the smell of ripe apples was left.

Say, that was one of the prettiest billfolds I had ever seen. I noticed it was made out of a very rich-looking leather that could have been goatskin, although maybe it was what leatherworkers call saddle leather; and it had a very pretty tooled design on it which was a galloping horse with wings. On the other side of the billfold were the initials F. E.

*   *   *

Well, what do you do with a woman's fancy billfold when you find it on the ground in a boys' outdoor dressing room? Do you open the billfold to see what's in it or do you just open it to see if a name is on the identification card in one of its clearview windows, which most billfolds have for the owner's name and address and for pictures of favorite friends?

Since Big Jim was the leader of our gang, Little Jim handed the billfold to him and right away Big Jim said, "It probably belongs to the turtledove that was here a little while ago looking for her high-heeled shoes. We'd better get dressed quick and take out after her and her bobwhite husband or brother, and see if we can find her and give the billfold back to her."

"What's her name?" Little Tom Till wanted to know, crowding in between Little Jim and me and turning his face sidewise so as soon as Big Jim would open it, he could read the name on the identification card in one of the windows.

"We don't need to know that," Big Jim said, but I noticed he decided to unzip the three-way zipper, and when he did the billfold flopped open like a four-page, leather-covered book. There were four swinging windows with a picture on each side of three of them. One of the windows had a card and the name on it was Frances Everhard. Then I got one of the most astonishing surprises I ever got in my life when Dragonfly, who was closest to Big Jim and looking over his elbow, exclaimed, "Why, she's got a picture of Charlotte Ann, Bill's baby sister!"

Boy, oh boy, you should have seen me crowd my way into the middle of our huddle to Big Jim's side to see what Dragonfly had thought he saw, and to my surprise I saw what looked like one of the cutest pictures of my baby sister, Charlotte Ann, I had ever seen. In fact, it was one I had never seen before and I wondered when Mom had had it taken and how on earth a barefoot woman, who dug holes in a cemetery at night, had gotten it.

Charlotte Ann in the picture was sitting in a fancy-looking high chair that had what looked like an adjustable footrest like they sell in the Sugar Creek Furniture Store. The food tray looked like it was shiny and was maybe made out of chrome. I remembered Mom had looked at one like that once in town and had wanted to buy it special for Charlotte Ann, but Dad had said the old one I had used when I was a baby, which was years and years ago, was good enough. It had made a husky boy out of me and besides he couldn't afford it—like he can't a lot of things Mom would like to buy and maybe knows she shouldn't because Dad is still trying to save money so he can buy a new tractor.

Also Charlotte Ann was wearing a very cute baby bonnet and a stylish-looking coat with a lot of lacy stuff around the collar. I didn't remember her having any outfit like that at all, although Mom could have bought it and had her picture taken one day in town when I hadn't known it.

She certainly had a cute expression on her face, which I had seen her have hundreds of times in my life. It looked like she was thinking some very mischievous thoughts and was trying to tell somebody what she was thinking and couldn't because she couldn't talk yet.

"It's *not* a picture of Charlotte Ann," Little Jim said, who managed to get his small, curly head in close enough to take a look. "She's got more hair than that."

Circus spoke up then and said, "Maybe it was taken about a year ago when she was a little smaller. She's bigger than that now."

There were other pictures of different people in the little clearview windows. Little Jim noticed there were several different-sized bills in the bill compartment—in fact, three fives and a ten and several ones, each one of the ones having on it a picture of George Washington, the first President of the United States; the fives, a picture of Abraham Lincoln; and the tens, one of Andrew Jackson.

Well, we brought it to a quick vote and the decision was to take the billfold up the path and start looking for the tent which the man and the woman were camping in and ask them if they had lost it.

As we moved along in a sort of half-worried hurry up the path toward the spring, I couldn't for the life of me think how on earth the barefoot woman could have gotten a picture of my baby sister. What would she want with it, anyway?

Well, maybe in the next fifteen minutes or so I would find out, but I was worried a little because, even as I followed along behind Poetry—all of us having to walk single file because the path through the tall weeds was narrow, just wide enough for one barefoot boy at a time—I was remembering that the woman was probably the same person who last night had been digging a hole in the old cemetery under the big pine tree beside Sarah Paddler's tombstone. I wondered what she had been digging in the earth for.

6

As I TOLD YOU, it was a terribly hot, sultry day, and over in the southwest sky a great big yellowish cumulus cloud was building up into a thunderhead. I knew from having lived around Sugar Creek for years and years that maybe before the day was over we would find ourselves in the middle of a whopper of a thunderstorm because that is the way the southwest part of the sky looks when it is getting ready to pour out about a million gallons of nice clean rainwater all over the farms around Sugar Creek.

Because Charlotte Ann's picture was in the pretty, brown, four-windowed billfold which Big Jim had zipped shut again, he let me carry it, which I did in the pocket of my overalls.

Boy, oh boy, it was hot and sultry even on the footpath, which was mostly shaded, on the way to the spring. Pretty soon we came to the spring itself, which as you know is at the bottom of an incline and has an old linden tree leaning out over it and shading it. Dad had made a cement reservoir, which was always full of the clearest water you ever saw. The water itself came singing out of an iron pipe, the other end of which Dad had driven away back into the rocky hill-side.

"Here are a woman's tracks again," Dragonfly said, looking down at the mud on the west side of the spring. My eyes followed his, expecting to see the print of a woman's high-heeled shoes. Instead I saw the print of a very small, bare foot with a narrow heel and five small toes, one of the toes being bigger than the rest, which meant that the woman had still been carrying her shoes when she had walked along here on the way back to her tent.

I noticed there was also a closed glass fruit jar in the spring reservoir with what looked like maybe a pound of yellow butter in it like the kind we churned ourselves at our house using an old-fashioned dasher churn, which I nearly always had to churn myself. I was even a better churner than Dad because some-times Dad would churn for twenty minutes and not get any butter and I could come in and churn for five minutes and it would be done that quick.

Say, that butter in the fruit jar meant that the man and woman were using our spring to get their drink-ing water and also to keep their butter from getting too soft—like Mom does at our house, only we keep ours in a fruit jar or a crock in the cellar instead.

Anyway, I thought, they wouldn't have to come to our house to get their drinking water out of our iron pitcher pump.

From the spring we went up the incline past the

elm sapling where Circus always likes to swing, and the linden tree with the friendly, lazy drone of the honeybees getting nectar from the sweet-smelling flowers. A linden tree as you know is the same as a basswood, and honeybees have the time of their lives when the clusters of creamy yellow flowers scatter their perfume all up and down the creek.

Going west from the tree, we followed a well-worn path toward the Sugar Creek bridge. Somewhere along that path off to the left we would probably find the tent because Old Man Paddler sometimes let people camp there for a few nights or a week if they wanted to under one of the spreading beech trees near the pawpaw bushes.

I kept my eyes peeled for the sight of a brown tent. As soon as we would see it we would go bashfully up to it and ask if anybody had lost a billfold. Then we would have them describe it to us and if it was like the one we had, we would give it to them. While we were there we would get a closer look at the small-footed woman who had been wearing overalls last night and had been digging in the cemetery. There would probably be an automobile also, since there had been one last night.

But say, we walked clear to the bridge and there wasn't even a sign of a tent anywhere.

Poetry got an idea then. "Let's go down to the old sycamore tree and through the cave up to Old Man Paddler's cabin and ask him. He'll know where their camp is. They couldn't camp here anyway without his permission."

So away we went on across the north road and along the creek till we came to the sycamore tree, which as you know is at the edge of the swamp not far from the cave. Pretty soon we were all standing in front of the cave's big wooden door, which Old Man Paddler keeps unlocked when he is at home because the cave is a shortcut to his cabin—the other end of the cave being in the basement of his cabin.

Big Jim seized the white doorknob like different ones of us had done hundreds of times. In a jiffy we would be in the cave's first room and on our way through the long, narrow passage to the cabin itself.

"Hey!" Big Jim exclaimed in a disappointed voice. "It's locked!"

I remembered that sometimes the old man had the door closed and locked for quite a while when he was going to be away, or when he was on a vacation, or maybe when he was writing something or other and didn't want any company.

We turned and went back to the spring again and on up the creek in the other direction to see if we could find the tent we were looking for.

After walking and looking around for maybe ten minutes without finding any tent, we came to another of Circus' favorite elm saplings near the rail fence which leads to Strawberry Hill. On the other side of the fence was Dragonfly's dad's pasture where there were nearly always a dozen cows grazing.

While we were waiting for Circus to get up the tree and down again I heard a rumbling noise a little like thunder mixed up with the sound of wind blowing. I looked up quick to the southwest sky expecting to see a rain cloud already formed and the storm itself getting ready to come pouring down upon us. But the big, yellow cumulus cloud was still where it had been, only it seemed a lot bigger, and some other queer-shaped clouds had come from somewhere to hang themselves up there beside it to keep it company. Those other clouds had probably carried a lot of their own rainwater to give to it so it would have enough to give our Sugar Creek farms a "real soaker," as Mom always called a big rain.

Then I looked over the rail fence into Dragonfly's dad's pasture and saw what looked like twenty scared cows racing furiously across the field, their tails up over their backs and also switching fiercely like the cows were terribly excited.

"It's a *stampede!*" Dragonfly cried excitedly.

Say, those cows acted like they were blind and deaf and dumb and scared out of what few wits a cow has and were all running wildly to get away from something—only I couldn't see anything for them to run away from.

"I'll bet it's a lot of warble flies after them," I said,

remembering what Dad and I had been studying that week while we were looking up June beetles.

"What's a warble fly?" Little Tom Till wanted to know, his folks not having any cows—and they always got the milk they drank at their house from Dragonfly's folks or mine.

Well, anybody who knows anything about a warble fly knows that it is a noisy, buzzing fly about half as big as a big black horsefly and it only lives six days after it is born.

"A warble fly doesn't have any mouth and can't sting or bite a cow or anything," I said, feeling all of a sudden quite proud that I had learned so much about a lot of important things such as flies and beetles and other insects.

"Then why are cows scared of them?" Poetry asked, even he not knowing that.

"They just make a fierce, buzzing sound and dive in and lay their eggs on the hair of the cows and as fast as the cows run they fly just that fast and flit in and out laying eggs on them. Then after six days of that kind of life they die. They probably starve to death," I said, "not being able to eat."

"And cows are scared of an innocent egg?" Circus asked, and just then got a little scared himself as did all of us because those twenty milk cows were making a beeline for our fence. "They're coming for the shade," I said. "Warble flies don't like shade."

And I was right, for a jiffy later in a cloud of whirling dust those twenty cows came to an excited halt under the maple tree just over the fence from us—only they didn't stay stopped but kept milling around, stamping their front feet and switching their tails madly, also doing the same kind of stamping with their back feet. It seemed like there were a lot of warble flies and I saw and heard some of them diving in and out under the cows, which kept on switching their tails fiercely and stamping their feet, which meant that if a boy had been there trying to milk one of them, he would have gotten the living daylights kicked out of him and his pail of milk spilled all over the ground or all over his clothes—and his parents would wonder what on earth had happened if they saw him like that.

Not getting any peace, those excited cows, still pestered with the flies, started on another stampede and this time it was toward the bayou and I knew that if they came to the weak place in the rail fence, where we sometimes climbed over, they would make a dive through it and rush into the brush and through the bushes and down the hill and in a jiffy would be in one of the sluggish ends of the bayou in the shade, which flies don't like. If the cows would stand up to their sides in the shady water, the warble flies would leave them alone because warble flies always lay their eggs on the legs and underparts of a cow.

"Hey!" Dragonfly exclaimed excitedly, being as worried as his dad probably would have been.

"They're going straight for the bayou!"

I knew if they did break through that fence and get into the water, they could also wade across and get into the cornfield on the other side and they might eat themselves to death like cows sometimes do.

Dragonfly grabbed up a stick and started out after the cows as fast as his spindly legs could carry him, which wasn't too fast. Circus, who was faster, was already dashing fiercely down the other side of the fence to get to the place which the cows were headed for.

I was running as fast as I could, following the gang —some of the gang following me—when I stepped into a brand new groundhog den, which I had never seen before, and down I went kerplop onto the ground. I was certainly surprised because there hadn't been any hole there before. I knew every groundhog den there was for a mile in every direction from our house.

Then I noticed the hole wasn't a groundhog den at all but another kind of hole. You could tell it hadn't been dug by any live, heavy-bodied, short-tailed, blunt-nosed, short-haired, short-legged, coarse-haired, grizzly brown animal with four toes and a stubby thumb on its two front feet and five toes on its two hind feet— which is what a groundhog is. Besides there wasn't any groundhog odor coming out of the hole, which my freckled nose was very close to right that second— and also there were the marks of a shovel and a woman's high-heeled shoes in the freshly dug soil.

7

I COULDN'T LET MYSELF stay there on the ground all sprawled out in five different directions wondering what had happened to me, because the gang had already gone and left me, running as fast as they could to catch up with and head off Dragonfly's dad's cows to keep them from breaking through the fence into the bayou, so I unscrambled myself, rolled over and up onto my feet and in a jiffy was helping the gang by running and yelling and screaming to the cows to obey us—which they didn't.

Even as I ran, I was remembering what Dad and I had learned about warble flies—or heel flies, as some folks call them—and I thought what if I was a real cow instead of merely being as awkward as one, part of the time? If I were a cow and had my own brain with what it knew about warble flies, I would have the living daylights scared out of me, even though a warble fly doesn't have any mouth and never eats any food during the six days of its short life, it does lay eggs all over the legs and lower part of the cow.

When a warble fly egg hatches, which it does in four or five days after it is laid, the thing that hatches out isn't a fly at all but a grub, which quick starts to bore its grubby way right through the cow's skin and into the cow. Once it gets inside, the dumb thing starts on a chewing journey through the inside, making its own path as it goes and making the cow itch like everything, which is maybe why some cows are not as friendly as other cows at certain times of the year. I'll bet if I were a cow, I wouldn't be worth a whoop to a farmer or anybody who owned me because I would probably feel the grub and maybe a half dozen or more of his grubby relatives working their way all through me, some of them stopping like grubs do, right in my throat and staying a while just above where I would be chewing my cud.

During the whole five or six months while a grub is still inside a cow, it travels all around and finally chews a tunnel along the edges of the cow's spinal column and at last it stops and makes its home right under the skin of the back. There it chews a small hole all the way through the cowhide so it can breathe, which it does with its tail, getting good fresh country air through the hole, staying there nearly through the winter.

While still there, the grub develops into a wiggling, twisting, squirming warble and finally works its way out through the air hole and tumbles off to the ground, and if it is spring and it doesn't get eaten up by a cowbird or a grackle or some other bird, it gets hard and black and finally changes into a fly. Then as quick as it is a fly, it makes a dive for the first cow it can find, starting to lay eggs as fast as it can before its six short days of noisy, buzzing life are over.

I was remembering all that as I galloped along after Dragonfly's dad's stampeding cows. I was also remembering that in the wintertime in some parts of America, starlings and even magpies light on the backs of cows and start pecking away on them, trying to dig out the warbles with their sharp bills.

Boy, oh boy, if I was a cow and one or a half dozen of those very high-voiced, buzzing flies was trying to lay her eggs on me and I knew what would happen if they did, I would most certainly beat it for the shade, which warble flies don't like. Or if I could, I would find somebody's bayou or a little stream somewhere, splash myself out into it and stand in the water up to my sides like I had seen cows do all around Sugar Creek for years without knowing before why they did it.

Say, you should have seen Dragonfly's dad's cows ignore the few rails on the fence when they got to it. They broke right through without stopping and disappeared in a tail-swishing hurry into the brush. By the time we got to the fence ourselves, those cows were down in the sluggish water of the pond at the east end of the bayou.

Maybe I'd better tell you that Dad says that every year American meat packers throw away enough grubby meat to feed eighty-three thousand people for a whole year—all because of the crazy warble flies. Also, Dad says a lot of cowhides have holes in them and people lose money that way too because that part of the cow is where the leather is generally best—and what good is a piece of leather for making shoes or leather goods if it has a hole in it? So a boy ought never to drive a bunch of cows out of a creek or a pond on a hot summer day, but should let them stay there in the shade if they want to.

Cows don't give as much milk while they are worrying about noisy, whining flies either, and beef cattle don't get fat as fast, it not being easy to get fat if you worry a lot, which is maybe why some people are too thin.

Anyway that is why we didn't get to look for the tent of the "turtledove" and the "bobwhite" until quite a while later. It took us almost an hour to get Dragonfly's dad's cows out of the bayou. We had to drive them out because the cornfield was on the other side, and you can't trust a cow with a cornfield any more than you can trust a boy or a girl with an open cookie jar.

If one of Dragonfly's dad's red heifers hadn't gotten a stubborn streak and decided she wanted to go on a wild run all through the woods, we might not have found the tent for a long time; but while we were chasing her all around through the bushes and up and down the creek, she accidentally took us right to it.

"It was swell of that old red heifer to show us where

the tent is, wasn't it?" Dragonfly said, after we had finally gotten her and the other cows back in Dragonfly's dad's dark cattle shed away from the flies, and we were back again not more than a hundred yards from the tent itself.

"Maybe the heifer smelled the calfskin in the folded billfold in Bill's hip pocket, and it scared her. Maybe she thought Bill wanted to make a lot of billfolds out of her hide," Little Tom Till said, trying to be funny.

Circus said, "I don't think heifers think."

One of the first things we noticed about the camp when we got close to it was that they had picked one of the very worst campsites in the whole woods. It was up in the middle of the woods, halfway between our house and the spring, away back off the barefoot boys' path so that I couldn't have seen it when I had gone galloping to the spring a couple of hours ago. It was under one of the biggest, widest-spreading oak trees around there anywhere and would have shade all day, which would mean it wouldn't get a chance to dry out after a damp night, which nights often are in any territory where there is a river or a creek or a lake. It wouldn't have any morning sun on it at all, like tents are supposed to have.

Any boy scout knows that nobody should ever pitch a tent under an oak tree because the droppings from an oak tree will make the canvas rot quicker and before you know it, you will have little holes scattered all over your roof, which will make it leak like everything when it rains. Also, I noticed, they had pitched the tent so the flap would be open toward the west. Anybody who lives at Sugar Creek knows that you shouldn't have the tent flap on the west side because that is the direction most of our rains come from.

Besides, they would have to go too far to get their drinking and cooking water—clear down to the spring or else in the opposite direction to the Collins family's iron pitcher pump.

"They certainly don't know very much about camp life," Big Jim said, having been a boy scout once. He had taught us all the different things about the best kind of campsite to pick.

"It's a good thing they got a shovel," Little Tom Till said, seeing one standing against an ironwood tree by their station wagon.

"Why?" Dragonfly said.

Little Tom Till answered, like a schoolboy who had studied his lesson and knew it by heart, "Because, where the tent's pitched now, if it rains, the water will run in from all sides and make a lake out of the floor."

Well, we brought it to a vote to see which one of us had to go up and knock on the tent pole and ask if anybody had lost a billfold.

It took only a jiffy for me to win the election by a six-to-one vote—six for me and one against me, my vote being the one that was against. So while the rest of the gang kept itself hidden behind some pawpaw bushes, I stepped out into the open and mosied along like I was only interested in seeing different things in the woods, such as a red squirrel in a tree or some kind of new beetle. Also I was walking carefully so as not to awaken them if they were asleep, especially the one who was supposed to take an afternoon nap.

Say, I forgot to tell you that tent wasn't any ordinary brown canvas tent, but was green and was a sort of three-way tent, shaped like some of the ranch houses that people were building in our town. I could tell just by looking at the tent that it would be wonderful for a gang of boys to go camping in. One of the wings of the tent was only a canvas roof with the sides made out of some kind of netting to keep out different kinds of flies, such as houseflies, deerflies and blowflies. It could even keep out a horsefly or a warble fly if one wanted to get in. It would also keep out June beetles at night.

Right away I saw somebody was resting on a cot inside one of the wings and as quick as that I was too bashful to go any closer because I could tell it was the woman herself lying there and she was maybe asleep, and it isn't polite to wake anybody out of a nap if you know he is taking one.

My heart was beating pretty fast because I was a little scared to do what I had been voted to do. But the man must have seen me or else heard all of us because right then he opened the flap of the main part of the tent and came out with the forefinger of one hand up to his lips and the other hand making the kind of motions a person's hand makes when he wants you to keep still and not say a word.

I noticed that the brownish-haired man was about as old as my reddish-haired dad and that he had a magazine in his hand like he had been reading. He also motioned for me to stop where I was, which I did and he kept on coming toward me with his finger still up to his lips and shaking a warning finger with his other hand, which meant "Shh—don't say a word."

I walked back with him to where the rest of the gang was behind the pawpaw bushes and I noticed that he had a very nice face. Also he looked like an important city person, who might be extra smart and maybe had charge of a big office or maybe a store or something.

"Is there anything I can do for you boys?" he said in a very deep-sounding voice.

Even though he had a half-sad look in his eyes, I could tell he was a kind person and probably liked boys.

I looked at Big Jim and he looked at me and we all looked at different ones of us. Finally the rest of the gang's twelve eyes focused on my freckled face and red hair so I looked up at the man and said, "Yes, sir. We found a billfold up along the creek—"

Little Tom Till cut in then and shouldn't have, saying, "Little Jim here found it and it's brown and has some dollar bills in it and three fives and one ten—"

"Shh!" Big Jim shushed Little Tom Till and the

man grinned with a twinkle in his eyes and I saw that the edge of one of his upper incisors had gold on it.

"That's all right. I can describe it for you," he said, which he did, giving all the details. "It has a tooled flying horse on the leather on the back and the initials F. E., and the name Frances Everhard in the inside on the identification card. The license number of our car is 734567. I was just ready to start looking for it."

There was something about the man that I liked although there was an expression in his eyes that made it seem like he was a little bit worried. I could tell he was the kind of man that would be kind to his wife— as Dad is to Mom. He might even be willing to do the dishes for her without being asked if she was extra-tired. I noticed he kept looking at Little Jim like he thought he was a very wonderful person.

"So you found it, did you, young man?" he asked.

"Yes, sir," Little Jim piped up in his mouselike voice.

"Well, I want to thank you. I have a reward for you. If you boys come back later, say in about an hour, my wife will wish to thank you in person. She has some cookies that she bought on purpose for you—just in case you happened to call to see us. She is having her nap now—doctor's orders are for her to sleep an hour every afternoon, you know."

We let the man have the billfold, which he took, and without opening it, shoved it into his hip pocket. "Frances will be so thankful. I think she doesn't know she lost it yet—and maybe we won't tell her, eh?"

We promised we wouldn't and he started to walk backward a little, which meant he was through visiting and we could go on home or somewhere.

"Wait," Mr. Everhard said and stopped as we also did because we had started in our own direction. "How would one of you boys like to earn a quarter every day by bringing our drinking water from the spring—or from up there at the Collins family house? One of you the Collins boy?"

I could feel myself blushing all over my freckled face, clear up to the roots of my red hair. I started to say yes, but Dragonfly beat me to it by saying, *"He* is," jerking his thumb in my direction.

The man stepped outside the tent and walked toward us. He went on to explain. "This isn't the best place to pitch a tent—so far from a water supply—but somebody told us the spring was your gang's meeting place so we decided to let you have your own privacy."

Big Jim was pretty smart, I thought, when he spoke up politely, "That was very thoughtful of you." Then he added with a Big Jim grin, "You'll probably have more privacy yourself up here away from the noisy spring"—meaning us. Then he added, "Sure, we will be glad to bring your drinking water every day, won't we, Bill?"

"Sure," I said to Big Jim. "I'll even help you carry it."

The man was almost halfway back to his tent when he stopped and hurried back to us again. "Mr. Paddler has given us permission to dig a few holes around here in the woods," he said, "so don't be too surprised if you find a new one every now and then."

I started to say, "What are you digging them for?" But I didn't because Big Jim scowled and shook his head at me.

A little later at the spring we stopped for a drink and Circus said, "Old Man Paddler doesn't own the cemetery. Who would give them permission to dig out there in the cemetery at night—and why would they want to do it?"

"Maybe they're studying different kinds of soil. Maybe they have a lot of glass jars full of different kinds of dirt in the tent or in the station wagon," Poetry suggested.

"They wouldn't need to dig such deep holes just to get soil samples," Big Jim said and I noticed he had a little bit of a worried look on his face.

Poetry had another idea. "How are we going to spend our quarter every day—the one Bill is going to earn for us?" That wasn't funny.

Our mystery wasn't any nearer solved than it had been. One reason why I felt quite disappointed was because I was sort of hoping that whoever had been digging in the cemetery the night before was what the police and detectives call a *ghoul*, which is a person who robs graves, and I was hoping that if it was such a person, maybe the gang could have a chance to help capture him or her.

Well, we had done all we could that afternoon although I was still wondering about the bobwhite whistle and the turtledove call. We talked that over while we were still at the spring and decided that maybe it was the way the man and his wife had of calling to each other—a sort of code or something—like we ourselves had. Whenever he wanted to call her, he could use the quail call and she could answer it by cooing like a turtledove. If that was the meaning of it, it was kind of nice and it showed that even married people could have fun together like my own mom and dad do a lot of times, in fact almost every day.

8

AT THE SUPPER TABLE at our house that night I think
I had never heard Mom and Dad laugh so hard. I was
still thinking about the warble flies that had scared
the living daylights out of Dragonfly's dad's cows. I
told them all about it, crowding my words out between bites, and I was crowding the bites in too fast
and shouldn't have. Dad said, "The heel flies are
pretty bad this year. Nearly every farmer in Sugar
Creek has been complaining about them. They have
been tormenting Old Brindle something fierce today.
I don't dare turn her out into the pasture without
leaving the gate into the barnyard open so she can
come rushing back in for the protection of the shade
anytime she wants to."

"Speaking of cows," Mom said, and her voice sort
of lit up like her face does when she has thought of
something very interesting or funny. "I read something in a farm magazine today that was about the
funniest thing I ever read in my life."

"What was it?" Dad said.

"Yes, what was it?" I said.

Dad and Mom were always reading things in magazines and telling them to each other and I didn't always get in on their jokes. Sometimes I had to ask them what they were laughing about and it didn't always seem as funny to me as it did to them. They also talked to each other about things that were not funny—things they had just that day learned about something in the Bible or something they had studied for next week's Sunday school lesson.

"I'll get it and read it for you," Mom said. She excused herself, left the table, went into the other room and came back with a small magazine. "It's a ten-year-old schoolgirl's essay on a cow."

Even before she started reading it I wasn't sure I was going to like it because I am close to being a ten-year-old boy myself and I could imagine what a ten-year-old girl would write on a cow.

Dad cleared his throat like he was going to read himself or else so he would be ready to laugh when the time came, and Mom started reading while Charlotte Ann wiggled and twisted on her high chair, she not being interested in anybody's essay on a cow. All Charlotte Ann was interested in about cows was the milk she had to drink three times a day and didn't always want to. So a story about a cow wouldn't be funny to her.

Even as I looked at Charlotte Ann I was remembering that there were plenty of unsolved things about our mystery. There was the picture of Charlotte Ann in the billfold; the strange-acting woman who had dug holes in a graveyard at night and had permission to dig them all over the Sugar Creek territory, who had to rest every afternoon, and who went barefoot and waded in the riffles all by herself—stuff like that. Why had she had the picture of Charlotte Ann in her billfold? The very second Mom got through reading and she and Dad got through laughing, I would ask her about the picture of Charlotte Ann.

Well, this is what Mom read, not getting to read more than a few lines before Dad interrupted her and the two of them started laughing. Dad stopped her maybe a half-dozen times before she finished and they laughed and laughed and kept on laughing and Mom wiped her tears and held her half-fat sides and Dad held his ordinary ones and I grinned and scowled.

This is what Mom read:

The cow is a mammal. It has six sides—right, left, up and below, inside and outside. At the back is a tail on which hangs a brush. With this it sends the flies away so they don't fall into the milk. The head is for the purpose of growing horns and so the mouth can be somewhere. The horns are to butt with and the mouth is to moo with. Under the cow, hangs the milk. It is arranged for milking. When people milk, the milk comes and there is never an end to the supply. How the cow does it I have never realized, but it makes more and more. The cow has a fine sense of smell, one can smell it far away. This is the reason for the fresh air in the country.

Well, that simply doubled up Mom and Dad in

laughter, and even Charlotte Ann pounded with her spoon on her ordinary wooden food tray, which I used to pound on years and years ago—the same spoon I had probably pounded with—and she acted like she was having the time of her life.

"What's the matter, Bill? Isn't it funny?"

"Not very," I said. "Anybody who is ten years old ought to know more about cows than that."

Right away Dad was ready to defend the girl by saying, "She was probably a city girl who didn't have any brothers," which also wasn't very funny.

"Say," I said to Mom, "have you had any new pictures taken of Charlotte Ann lately?"

"Why, no. Why do you ask?"

"You haven't had one taken of her sitting in that fancy high chair in the Sugar Creek Furniture Store?"

"Why, no. Why do you ask?"

"Oh, I just wondered." I had made up my mind not to tell her any more.

As soon as supper was over, I started to do the dishes without being asked to for a change, almost enjoying it because I was learning to enjoy doing things for Mom when she was tired. In fact, it makes me feel fine inside—almost as good as I feel when I am eating a piece of ripe watermelon—to do the dishes while she rests, because she is a pretty swell mom.

Dad was in the other room with Mom, talking to her while she rested. Mom was actually lying down while she was doing it, she was that tired.

"The most friendly couple is camping down in the woods," I heard Mom say. "They were here this afternoon a little while. She's the prettiest thing I think I ever saw—kind of fancy though, and wearing high-heeled shoes—not at all the kind an experienced camper or hiker would wear. They wanted a pail of well water and I sold them a pound of Old Brindle's butter, which they are going to keep cool in the spring."

Hearing Mom say that, I sidled over to the kitchen door with her apron on and the drying towel in my hands and listened to what else she was saying. I got there too late to get all of it. "She's just out of the hospital, he told me. She doesn't look like there's a thing in the world wrong with her, but her husband—their name is Everhard—says she is under special treatment and she has been released to him. She's not at all dangerous, but she gets depressed at times, and sometimes right in the middle of the night she gets one of her spells."

I heard Dad sigh and say, "Being out here in the country with plenty of fresh air and good country food with an understanding husband like that will be good for her. I wonder how long she has been that way."

Mom said, "He told me confidentially when she was out in the car that it started about a year ago. She's all right when she's all right, but these spells come on and she cries—but she never does anything desperate—only wants to go around digging holes in the ground."

That was as much as I got to hear right then because the phone rang and when Dad answered, it was Little Jim's mom, the pianist at the Sugar Creek church, wanting to talk to Mom about something or other.

Mom was always tickled when it was Little Jim's mom calling because Little Jim's mom was her best friend and sometimes they talked and talked until one of them had to quit because she smelled something burning on the stove.

Well, I, the maid of the Collins family, went back to the kitchen to slosh my hands around a little longer in the hot sudsy water. Seeing our battery radio on the utility table and wondering what program was on, I wiped the water from my right hand and turned on the radio, dialing to a station that sometimes had a story for boys at that time. I tuned in just in time to hear the deep-voiced announcer in a terribly excited hurry say something about "those red dishpan hands" and then he galloped on to tell all the women listeners to be sure to use a certain kind of fancy-named soap that would make their hands soft and pretty almost right away. The soap was also good for washing dishes.

Dad had to come through the kitchen on his way to the barn, so he stopped and listened with me. Then he said, "You using the right kind of soap, son?"

"I don't know. I hope so, but I'm afraid I *am* getting dishpan hands. Look at 'em!" I held my hands out for him to look at and he said with a mischievous grin in his voice, "Looks like you got dishpan hair too." Then he turned the radio down a little saying, "Your mother is resting, so keep it low."

"She's talking on the phone," I said.

"It's the same thing. You will find out she will be all full of pep when she gets through," which I knew might be the truth because Mom nearly always felt fine when she finished listening and talking to Little Jim's mom, who was always cheerful on the telephone.

"She smiles with her voice," Mom always said about Little Jim's mom.

Dad went on out to the barn with the milk pail to see if the warble flies had tormented Old Brindle so much that day that she didn't have time to manufacture as much milk as usual, and I went on back to my half-cold dishwater.

I was just finishing washing the last dish and was getting ready to start wiping them when Mom finished talking and listening to Little Jim's mom. But say, when she came in she was still tired. She sighed as she lifted the steaming teakettle and poured water over the dishes so she could dry them easier.

All of a sudden I got a half-sad, half-glad feeling in my heart, so I said to her, "You go on back in the other room and rest some more. I'm getting along swell." I suppose I was glad because for a change I actually wanted to help her and maybe I was sad be-

74

cause Mom's sighs nearly always make me feel that way for some reason.

She sighed again and started in helping me. I decided to let her because I didn't want to discourage her from helping a tired-out son with his work.

She was so quiet for about three minutes, while all we could hear was the lazy ticking of the old clock on the mantel and the sound of the plates and cups and saucers and silverware. Pretty soon Mom said, still sadly, "I feel so sorry for her. Poor thing. If only she could believe and trust in God!"

I heard myself sigh the same kind of sigh Mom had sighed and felt sorry for the woman myself—knowing whom Mom meant. Then I guess Mom had decided that I ought to know more about Mrs. Everhard. First she told me some things I never knew about the Collins family itself, using a kind of sad voice and saying, "I want you to know before you get any older. It will help you to understand your mother and father better, and all other people who have had to bury a little baby."

"What?" I thought, without saying a word. Mom's voice sounded different than I had ever heard it as she went on. "Just two years before you were born, Bill, your father and I had to give back to God a very beautiful little three-week-old baby girl. She was so very lovely and sweet and it broke our hearts, but we have tried to thank Him that He let us have her to love even for such a little while." Mom stopped and again all we could hear was the lonely clock that was ticking so sadly it seemed like it must have felt sorry for Mom too.

Mom, still being very serious, went on. "Then God gave us you to take her place and you have been a great joy to us." Again she stopped.

I knew that if all her thoughts had come out in words, she could have added, "And also a lot of trouble." But Mom didn't and I liked her even better, taking a sidewise glance up at her out of the corner of my eye.

I guess maybe I had seen my mother's face a million times—and while it's nearly always the same, I have never gotten tired of looking at it. She always looks just like my mom even when she's all tired out or sad and hasn't had time to powder her nose from the hard work she is doing in the kitchen or out in the garden or orchard or somewhere.

"She's a pretty wonderful mom," I thought and swallowed something in my throat which stopped a couple of tears from getting into my eyes. Then I began working a little harder and faster on the dishes, which I had decided to help dry.

A little later Mom told me something else about the strange woman and her husband, who were camping down in the Sugar Creek woods—something Little Jim's mom had just told her over the phone. Something had happened to the woman's mind, which the doctors called by some kind of fancy name, which meant she was mentally ill and maybe would be for a while until she had time to get well again.

"Thousands of people get well from being mentally ill," Mom explained, "just like children do from such things as chicken pox and whooping cough. Sometimes though they have to have very special treatment in a special hospital."

"I can understand how she feels," Mom went on, "because for a long time after we had buried little Nancy it seemed like she couldn't possibly be dead. She *had* to be alive, I kept thinking, and I kept imagining I could hear her crying in the other room."

"In there where Charlotte Ann is now?" I asked.

Mom didn't answer for a minute. She only nodded and sighed again. Then she said, "I never actually heard her voice, of course. And that is what is wrong with the dear little mother who is camping down there in the woods. You boys be very careful to be very kind and—"

"Is she an honest-to-goodness crazy woman?" I asked and shouldn't have. Mom replied, "Thoughtful people never say that anymore about a person who is ill in the way Mrs. Everhard is. They always say that they are not well *emotionally*. We try to understand them and to find out what made them that way, and sometimes when they themselves come to understand what caused their illness they begin to get well right away—in fact, some of them get well almost at once. Doctors try to give them something to hope for. It was only the grace of God and my believing in Him that spared me from going to pieces myself," Mom said. "He gave your father and me strength to stand the loss of your baby sister Nancy."

Say, when Mom said "your *sister*," I did get a lump in my throat because I was thinking what if it had been Charlotte Ann who had died.

"You boys must not act surprised when you find those little, freshly dug holes here and there in the woods or along the creek because when she gets one of her sad spells she imagines her baby is still alive, even though it was buried, and she starts digging a hole in the woods or along the creek, looking for it. She thinks it was buried alive when she feels like that. She will dig awhile and then stop to listen to see if she can hear it crying."

When Mom said that I was remembering that we had seen her do that very thing in the old cemetery last night.

"Couldn't the doctors make her well?" I asked Mom.

"Not with just medicine alone. One thing the doctor has prescribed for her is that she attend some church regularly—a church where the minister believes and preaches the Bible and what it teaches about heaven and the wonderful place it is, and how people can meet their loved ones there, alive and well—all through trusting in the Saviour. The doctor thinks that if Mrs. Everhard can learn to trust in God and to believe that she will see her baby again, she will be cured."

9

WELL, IT SEEMED after that wonderful talk with Mom that I, Bill Collins, was going to be a better boy than I had ever been in my life before—although I didn't see how I could change all of me so quick. Anyway I thought I knew why Mom every now and then sighed even when I couldn't see a thing to sigh about. Maybe a sad thought came to her that wasn't caused by the hot weather or from being all tired out or because I might have been a bad boy, which I sometimes used to be.

Several weeks went by during which the gang found maybe twenty-five different-sized holes in different places in the woods and along the creek. Also we were not surprised when most anytime we heard a quail call and a turtledove answer it. Sometimes though it was the woman who gave the quail call and the man was the turtledove who answered.

It began to be almost fun to hear them because we could tell that they liked each other a lot. They were kind of like a gang themselves only there were only two of them and their whistling to each other was like a game of some kind—just like we ourselves played different kinds of games. It was like having a secret code. They wanted us all to stop at their green tent every day and nearly always Mrs. Everhard had something for us to eat, which made it easy to remember to stop. Of course, I had to go anyway to carry water from our iron pitcher pump to them.

Each Sunday the Everhards came to our church to hear our minister, who in nearly every sermon mentioned something about heaven and how to get there—such as when you know in your heart that you are an honest-to-goodness sinner and that you can't save yourself—which nobody can—and if you trust the Saviour Himself to forgive all your sins, you will be sure to go there; and all the babies that ever died are already there because the blood of Jesus Christ shed upon the cross took care of all of them—things like that.

I had to watch myself to keep from looking across the church all the time to watch Mrs. Everhard to see if she was believing the sermon. The only thing was, instead of looking at the minister, she kept looking at Mom or Dad or me, whichever one of us was holding Charlotte Ann, like she wondered if we were taking care of her right.

One Sunday right in the middle of the sermon she quick stood up and walked down the aisle in a hurry to the outside door, and her husband after her. A little later I heard through the open window the station wagon motor start and I knew he was taking her back to the tent quick, she maybe having left so she wouldn't cry in church.

That afternoon when Dad was helping our minister and some other men hold a jail meeting and Mom and I were alone, Mr. Everhard came over to our house to borrow Charlotte Ann a while.

"*Borrow* her!" Mom said with an astonished voice and face.

He answered, "Yes, Charlotte Ann looks so very much like our own little Elsa used to look that I thought if Frances could hold her a while and listen to her as she pretends to talk it might make her feel better. She's very much down today."

Well, I had heard of people borrowing nearly everything else. Around Sugar Creek the gang's different mothers borrowed different kinds of kitchen things, which they sometimes ran out of and had to have in a hurry—as fast as a boy could run to the neighbors and get it. Sometimes Dragonfly's dad borrowed our brace and bit or Dad's hand drill or keyhole saw; and Dad would sometimes borrow them back again if he needed them in a hurry—I getting to run to Dragonfly's house to get them—and not getting to stay and play with Dragonfly, which made it a very hard errand to be sent on. Also different members of the gang would borrow knives or fishhooks or bobbers or other things from each other.

But whoever heard of anybody borrowing a baby? I could see Mom wasn't going to like the idea and if she didn't I wasn't going to either, but because she felt so sorry for the lady and wanted her to get well fast, she quick thought up a way to say yes without hurting Mr. Everhard's feelings or her own.

"If you will borrow me too, that will be fine," she said cheerfully, and he answered, "Certainly, it will soon be time for afternoon tea anyway."

"What about *me?*" I said, all of a sudden trying to be funny and probably not being very. "Anybody want to borrow a good-looking, red-haired, homely faced boy?" I didn't really want to go though because some of the gang might come over to play with me.

But Mom said quickly, "Certainly, son, come right along."

And so it turned out that I went with Mom and Charlotte Ann and Mr. Everhard, carrying a gallon thermos jug of cold water to earn my twenty-five cents for that day.

Say, the first thing I noticed when we came to within a few yards of the green canvas, ranch-house-style tent was that one of the tent's wings with the green roof and the mosquito netting sidewalls had in it a baby's playpen, and in the pen were a lot of things for a baby girl to enjoy—a doll, a pink teddy bear, a very small broom like the one Charlotte Ann helps Mom sweep with, and a little tea set for playing house. Beside the tent, hanging by a rope and a spring, was a jumper swing like the one that used to hang from the limb under the plum tree in our yard in which

Charlotte Ann used to sit and bounce herself up and down and laugh and gurgle and have the time of her life—but now it's too little for her.

"The poor, dear girl," Mom said with a sigh under her breath and in my direction—Mr. Everhard having gone on into the tent to tell his wife she had company. Mom was looking at the baby things with a sort of faraway expression in her eyes. I could hear voices inside the tent and it sounded for a minute as if there was a half argument. Then the canvas flap of the tent opened and Mrs. Everhard came out.

Mom gasped when she saw her, because of the way she was dressed and what she had in her hand.

"Such a pretty dress," Mom said, half to me and half to nobody.

I hardly ever paid any attention to what anybody was wearing, especially a woman or a girl, because it didn't seem important, but I guess any woman or maybe even a boy would gasp at the green and brown and yellow and red summery-looking dress Mrs. Everhard had on. It had a lot of milkweed flowers on it with pretty swallowtail butterflies with spread wings on each flower. Her yellowish hair was the same color as the sulphur butterflies that fly around our cabbage plants with the white ones, and I noticed it was still combed like it had been in church, with some kind of sparkling pin in it. She was wearing a pair of dark glasses and green and yellow shoes.

To my tangled-up surprise she had in her hands a

shovel like the one she had been using to dig in the ground. She looked all around in a sort of dazed circle, not seeing us at first, then she started off in a hurry in the direction of Strawberry Hill.

Say, quick as anything and without knowing I was going to do it, I whistled a sharp bobwhite whistle that flew as straight as an arrow right toward her. It made her stop stock-still and stand and stare. Then her eyes fell on Charlotte Ann, whom Mom had dressed special for the visit in a little blue organdy playsuit that made her look as cute as a bug's ear and even cuter.

Say, Frances Everhard dropped her shovel like it had had a hot handle and gasped an excited gasp like women who like babies do when they see a pretty one, and said, "You *darling* baby!" She started to make a beeline for her, like she was going to pick her up, then she stopped, whirled around fast and disappeared into the tent.

For just a second I had a queer fluttering feeling in my heart and it was kind of like about fifty pretty black and yellow swallowtail butterflies had been fluttering in front of my eyes in the bright sunlight and then all of a sudden had flown toward the green tent and disappeared all at once. It was the same kind of happy feeling I get when I heard a wood thrush singing but can't see it and wish I could.

A jiffy later she was back outside again with a camera. For a while she didn't act like anybody was around except Charlotte Ann. Her extrapretty face was all lit up and she seemed very happy. "She looks almost enough like my own Elsa to be a twin," she told Mom. "In fact, almost enough to *be* her." Then she sighed a heavy sigh and so did Mom.

* * *

Well, it was a very interesting visit we had that afternoon at the ranch house tent. As soon as Charlotte Ann got over being a little bit bashful, she let Mrs. Everhard hold her and take all kinds of pictures of her: in the playpen, in the jumper swing, lying on a blanket and doing different things. She had her bobwhite husband take a picture of the two of them while she held Charlotte Ann on her lap.

Everybody had a good time except me because I like to keep my mind in a boy's world, and nobody could do that when there were three grownups and a baby around. So I asked if they would like me to get some fresh, cold water from the spring and when they said yes I took a thermos jug and shot like a red-headed arrow out past the pawpaw bushes toward the old overhanging linden tree above the spring.

I was thinking as I ran that the mystery of the little holes being dug all over Sugar Creek territory was all explained and it looked like the gang would have to scout around for some other problem to set our seven different kinds of brains to working on. I didn't know as I ran that because Charlotte Ann and the woman's dead baby looked so much alike I was going to have to put my own brain to work in a very special way before the summer was over.

*　　*　　*

I guess I never realized before just how wonderful a person I had for a baby sister until I thought I was going to lose her. As quick as I can, I will start telling you all about it. First though I have to tell you something else about her because some of the people who will read this story don't know much about her and it will help them understand how come she got lost.

We always had more fun than you can shake a stick at, taking care of Charlotte Ann at our house, in spite of the times when she was a nuisance. Dad especially had a lot of fun because he nearly always had to put her to bed at night—that is, after she was a little bigger than a little baby. Going to bed was one of the things Charlotte Ann liked even worse than she liked anything else—after she got to be about two years old. Before that we didn't have to worry about her getting all the sleep she needed because she would go to sleep anywhere, any place and nearly any time, but all of a sudden she was a two-year-old and seemed to have ideas of her own about such things as going to bed at night and taking afternoon naps.

"That is because at two," Mom said—after reading a book on how to take care of babies at that age—"they are great *imitators*. Whatever they see you do they want to do too. They like to do grownup things before they are old enough or strong enough or have sense enough to."

"Or sense enough *not* to," Dad said and Mom agreed with him, both of them seeming to think it was funny. But I couldn't understand what they meant.

"Also," Mom said, "a two-year-old has to have twelve hours of sleep at night and at least one hour in the afternoon of every day." She was talking to me at the time. "You had to have it when you were a baby and we saw to it that you got it whether you wanted it or not—which you generally didn't—and see what a wonderfully fine, strong boy it made out of you!"

I got a mischievous streak when she said that and answered, "I can see how maybe I am a wonderful boy and very fine but I feel very *weak* right now." She had just a jiffy before ordered me to carry in a couple of armfuls of wood for the woodbox, which never seemed to have sense enough to stay full and always managed to get itself empty at the very time I didn't want to fill it and generally when I wanted to do something else.

"See," I said to Mom, "before you asked me to get that wood I could swing both arms up over my head and still feel fine—just like this." I held my arms over my head like I was as strong as the imaginary man named Atlas who used to hold the world on his shoulders. "But now," I went on to Mom, "I'm so weak I can't lift my right arm more than this high, just about as high as my waist, I am so weak."

I had heard Little Jim's dad say and do that to Little Jim's mom once and it had sounded cute so I had decided to try it on my parents the first chance I got.

Mom, who was getting dinner at the time, stopped stirring the gravy, turned and looked through the lower part of her bifocals at me and said, "Poor boy. That's too bad. If you can't lift your hand any higher than your waist how then can you carry in the wood! I'll take care of the wood myself. Maybe you'd better go and lie down for an hour while your father and I have dinner because, your mouth being a little higher than your waist, you won't be able to feed yourself." For some reason I right away went out and carried in several armloads of wood without saying another word, getting it done about the same time Mom had dinner ready.

But let me get back to telling you about Charlotte Ann and how she got mixed up in our mystery. The worst trouble we had with her was that when we finally got her into bed at night or in the afternoon when it was her nap time she didn't want to go to sleep. Sometimes she would call for a drink of water or something to eat and sometimes she would come toddling out in her bare feet to wherever Mom and Dad and I were, and interrupt our reading or our talking or Dad's evening nap on the davenport. She nearly always came out wide awake acting very friendly and like she felt more at home when she was up than when she was down.

"What on earth makes her want to do that?" I said one day. "Doesn't she have sense enough to stay in bed?"

"She's lonesome," Mom answered. "She's awful lonesome and she has to have lots of attention. You were that way when you were little."

"Oh, quit telling me about when I was little years and years ago," I said, not wanting to even be reminded that I ever had been a baby.

As I started to say, getting Charlotte Ann to bed was a hard problem. It got to be my job to help Mom make her go, when Dad had to be away.

But when Mom and Dad were both away, then I had to do it all by myself—being the babysitter.

One very hot afternoon Mom and Dad both had to be gone for two or three hours and so they let me stay home to take care of Charlotte Ann, giving me orders to see to it that she took her afternoon nap between 1:30 and 2:30, or as near to that as I could get her to; and if it rained, to close all the windows—things like that.

"Take good care of her," Mom said, as she looked out the closed car door window, all dressed up in her Sunday dress.

"I will," I promised and she and Dad went spinning out through the front gate, past "Theodore Collins" on the mailbox and onto the highway—their car stirring up a big cloud of white dust that moved slowly off in the direction of Bumblebee Hill and the old cemetery.

10

I shut the gate after Mom and Dad, and Charlotte Ann and I went hand in hand toward the house to take her nap. That is, her hand was in mine—she not wanting it to be there because she knew it was nap time and she didn't want to take one.

"It's not hard to take a nap," I said to her. "You just lie down and shut your eyes and that's all there is to it. I'm the babysitter and you are the baby-lying-downer. My first job is to get you to bed, so here we go."

I was using a very cheerful voice, but she seemed to be suspicious of such a voice coming from me. Besides she was still a little tearful from Mom and Dad having gone and left her at home with me.

I realized that I was going to have to use one of Dad's tricks to get her to want to go to bed—one he used sometimes at night. I had seen him put her to bed maybe a hundred times so I looked down at her and said cheerfully, "OK, kid. Let's get going."

I was surprised at how easy it was at first. It didn't take long to get her ready because Mom had said she could rest in her playsuit, which Mom called her sunsuit. Just like Dad does, I pretended to be a poor, crippled, old grandfather, saying to her with a, trembling voice like I was suffering terribly, "I've got to get into that other room and I need somebody to help me walk."

I started limping terribly bad toward the room where she was supposed to sleep, going very slowly like a very crippled old man, staggering and limping and whining and complaining.

If there is anybody she likes better than anybody else, it is Old Man Paddler. She must have imagined that I was him because quick as anything she made a dive in my direction, clasped her small hand around my right knee and held on tight while I limped the best I could with one leg and walked the best I could with the other. We struggled toward the room where her small bed was. All the way there I kept on complaining with a trembling old voice saying, "Poor old man. How can I walk without a nice little girl to help me?"

The very minute we got to her bed—the green window shade being down and it being almost dark—she must have decided to do like she does when it is night when she always says her prayers before getting into bed. Right away she was down on her knees making me get down beside her. I bent my poor, old rheumatic knees down to the hard floor; and without waiting for me to say anything, she started in in her babyish voice trying to say the prayer Dad had been teaching her:

93

Now I lay me down to sleep.
  I pray Thee, Lord, my soul to keep.
If I should die before I wake,
  I pray Thee, Lord, my soul to take.
For Jesus' sake. Amen.

It was the same prayer I used to say myself years and years ago. Sometimes even yet when I kneel down to say a good-night prayer to God and I am very tired and sleepy, before I know it I am saying it myself even though I am too big to say just a little poem prayer.

As quick as her prayer was finished, I swooped her up and flip-flopped her into bed, but for some reason or other she was as wide awake as anything. She didn't stay lying down, but sat straight up in bed with a mischievous grin all over her cute face. She was the most wide-awake baby I ever saw.

"I want my dolly," she ordered me in her own language, which is what she always does at night.

"OK," I said, getting it for her from somewhere in the other room where I found it upside down lying on its face. I handed it to her.

"I want my rag dolly too," she said.

"OK I'll get your dirty-faced rag dolly." I went to the corner of the room where it was lying on its side with its left foot stuck in its face. I carried it to her and tossed it into the bed with her where it socked her in the cheek, but didn't hurt. Then I said, "OK now. Go to sleep." I was halfway to the door when she called again saying, "I want my 'puh' "—meaning her little pink dolly pillow.

I came back and sighed down hard at her and started looking everywhere for her pink pillow, wondering what else she would want and why. I soon found out because next she wanted her hanky, a pretty colored handkerchief which Dad had had to get for her every night all summer and which she always held up close to her face when she went to sleep, it being very soft. Mom said, "She likes to feel secure and all these things help her to feel that way. She imagines the dollies are honest-to-goodness people and she feels she isn't alone when they are with her in bed, and they keep her from being afraid."

I couldn't help but think that Poetry, who as you know is always quoting a poem, if he were there, would probably quote one by Robert Louis Stevenson, which goes like this:

> In winter I get up at night
>   And dress by yellow candlelight.
> In summer quite the other way
>   I have to go to bed by day.

For some reason or other as I looked down at her cuddling her dollies, I think I had never liked her so well in my whole life—even though I was still half disgusted with her for making me carry so many things to her. I guess I was a little worried, though, which probably helped me to like her better. I kept thinking about the woman who had been digging holes in the earth who thought Charlotte Ann looked enough like her own dead Elsa to be her twin—in fact, enough like her to *be* her. I wished the woman would hurry up and get well, but she didn't seem to be improving very much because the gang had kept on finding new holes all around Sugar Creek.

Pretty soon Charlotte Ann's eyes went shut and stayed shut and her regular breathing showed that she was asleep.

Realizing that at last she was asleep, I went out through the living room into the kitchen and through that. Out of doors, I closed the screen door more quietly than it had been closed for a long time and went on out toward the iron pitcher pump—suddenly being very thirsty.

Halfway to the pump I stopped on the boardwalk and turned around to see if anything was wrong, feeling something was, because nearly always by the time I got that far out of doors I heard the screen door slam behind me, but this time it hadn't done it and it was a little bit confusing to me not to hear it.

Babysitting was hard work, I thought, and it would be silly to do two long hours of it actually sitting down.

A few tangled-up jiffies later I was up on our grape arbor in a perfect position for eating a piece of pie upside down but I didn't have any pie so I couldn't babysit that way.

Pretty soon I was tired of being up on that narrow two-by-four crossbeam, so I wriggled myself down and walked over to the water tank on the other side of the pump where a lot of yellow butterflies, seeing me come, made a scramble in different fluttering directions. Then right away the air was quiet again as they settled themselves down all around the edge of a little water puddle.

Maybe I could get Dad's insect book and look up a new insect for him. Maybe I could look up something about yellow butterflies which laid their eggs on Mom's cabbage plants and also the green larvae, which hatched out and ate the cabbages. But I wasn't interested in getting any more education just then.

Spying my personally owned hoe leaning against the toolhouse on the other side of the grape arbor, an idea popped into my head—and out again quick—to do a few minutes' babysitting by hoeing a couple of rows of potatoes in the garden just below the pignut trees near which Dad had buried Old Addie's two red-haired pigs; but for some reason or other I began to feel very tired and I could tell it would be very boring to babysit that way.

I mosied along out to where Old Addie was doing her own babysitting near a big puddle of water beside her apartment house, lying in some straw that was still clean. She was acting very lazy and sleepy and grunting while her six red-haired, lively youngsters were having a noisy afternoon lunch.

"Pretty soft," I said down to her but she didn't act like she even recognized me.

I was remembering a silly little rhyme which I had heard in school when I was in first grade.

> Six little pigs in the straw with their mother,
>> Bright-eyed, curly-tailed, tumbling on each other.
>
> Bring them apples from the orchard trees,
>> And hear those piggies say, "Please, please, please."

That gave me an idea so I scrambled out to the orchard, picked up six apples and brought them back. Leaning over the fence I called out, "Here, piggy, piggy, piggy. Here are some swell apples. Say please and you can have them."

But they ignored me, not only not saying please but probably not even saying thank you in pig language to their mother.

So I tossed my six apples over into the hog lot where they rolled up to the open door of Addie's apartment, and that was the end of her six babies' afternoon lunch. She shuffled her heavy body to her feet, swung it around and started in on those apples like she was terribly hungry.

"Well, what next?" I thought and wondered if Old Bentcomb, my favorite white hen, who always laid her egg in the nest up in our haymow, had laid her egg yet today. It was too early to gather the eggs, but I could get hers if she had it ready.

Into the barn and up the ladder I went and there she was, with her pretty white neck and head and her long red bent comb hanging down over her right eye like a lock of brown hair drops down over the right eye of one of Circus' many sisters, who even though she is ordinary-looking doesn't act like she thinks I am a dumbbell like some girls do that go to the Sugar Creek school.

"Hi, Old Bentcomb," I said, but she ducked her head and ignored me.

"Pretty soft life," I said. "You don't have to worry about taking care of a baby sister while your parents are away."

Down the ladder I went and shuffled back across the barnyard thinking maybe it would be a good idea to peek in under the window shade to see if Charlotte Ann was still asleep.

11

As I TOLD YOU, it was one of those terribly hot after-
noons and the Collins family had been hoping for a
week that it would rain because our crops needed a
real soaker. Just to find out for sure if it was going to,
I lifted up a little wooden step at the door on the
north side of our house to see if a smooth, round stone
that was half buried there was wet, which it always is
when it is going to rain. Dad looks there himself
when he wants to find out whether it will rain—and
Mom teases him about it.

The minute the daylight streamed into where the
dark had been under that step, a lot of different kinds
of bugs scrambled for a dark place to hide. I noticed
especially that there was a big, black cricket, maybe
the very one that sings every night just outside Mom's
and Dad's bedroom window—which Mom says sings
her to sleep. She likes to hear crickets but isn't interested in looking at them or touching them.

The smooth, round stone was wet, I noticed, which
meant that there was a lot of humidity in the air.
Then I put the step back down again and went to the
corner of the house to look to see if there was a big

yellowish cloud in the southwest and there was, so it might rain before night, I thought.

Just that second I saw a large, tiger-colored swallow-tail butterfly out by the orchard fence, fluttering around a red thistle blossom. Because the swallowtail is one of the largest kinds of butterflies in our whole territory, I knew Dad would be especially tickled if I could catch one for our collection. So I quick circled the house to the toolshed, swished in, swooped up Dad's butterfly net—and a jiffy later was out by the orchard fence where the most beautiful butterfly I had ever seen was acting like the nectar of that big bull thistle blossom was about the sweetest thing in the world to eat.

Generally we didn't allow any bull thistles to grow on our farm. But because Dad knew that swallowtail butterflies like milkweed and thistle flowers better than any others, we had let this one grow, hoping a swallowtail would decide to live around our place because it is one of the prettiest sights a boy ever sees on a farm—a beautiful butterfly drifting around and lighting on the flowers, its different-colored wings folding and unfolding and making a boy feel all glad inside.

The swallowtail was on the other side of the woven wire fence, which was very hard to climb over, so I quick hurried to the orchard gate near the cherry tree. I got to the thistle just as the gorgeous yellow and black swallowtail decided to leave, floating lazily along like a feather in the wind, with me right after it, swinging my net at it and missing it, and running and getting hot—and still not catching it.

Then all of a sudden I heard a quail's whistle. I stopped stock-still and looked all around, expecting to see either Mr. Everhard or his wife. A jiffy later I saw which one it was and it was *Mr.* Everhard. I wanted to give a mournful turtledove call to answer him, but instead I listened for his wife to answer, which she didn't.

Seeing me, he called to me saying, "Have you seen anything of Mrs. Everhard?"

"No, I haven't," I called back, deciding to forget about the swallowtail I was after—besides when I had taken my eye off the butterfly I had lost it.

"She was taking her afternoon nap," Mr. Everhard said, "so I had gone to the creek a while, but when I came back she was gone. You sure she's not up at your house?"

"I'm sure," I said and I suddenly remembered that it had been a long time since I was inside our house. Also for some reason I decided I had better go quick to see if Charlotte Ann was still asleep or if she had waked up and maybe had gone somewhere herself.

"Let's go look," I said to Mr. Everhard and started to run fast, with him right after me.

All the way through the orchard to the big bull thistle and the gate, not bothering to wait for Mr. Everhard, I was thinking over and over, "Mrs. Everhard had been taking a nap while her husband was away and when he came back she was gone and he couldn't find her—gone and he couldn't find her—and she was crazy—emotionally ill and—and our Charlotte Ann looked enough like her dead baby, Elsa, to be her twin—enough like her to *be* her."

I tried to run faster and couldn't. Instead of flying along like a bird in a hurry, I felt that I was just crawling like a swallowtail butterfly's ugly, reddish-brown larva crawling along a lance-shaped parsnip leaf in our garden—which is the kind of leaf a swallowtail's larva likes to eat best.

Hurry! Hurry! Hurry! If ever I hurried, I hurried then.

I darted past the big red, two-inch-wide thistle blossom, not even stopping to glance at it to see if there might be another swallowtail fluttering around it, through the still-open gate and past the front doorstep, around the house, past the grape arbor to the back screen, which I remembered now I hadn't locked from the outside like I should have.

She's got to be there, I thought. Why, she could have toddled out that door and gone to the barn or even through the front gate and across the dusty road and through the woods to the spring and the creek *and she didn't know how to swim!*

She didn't know how to swim!

Then I thought what if Mrs. Everhard had gotten one of her spells and decided that Charlotte Ann really *was* her baby and had come to get her and had run away with her—*kidnapped her.* She *had* to be there in her crib asleep—*had* to be!

I made a barefoot dash through the kitchen and the living room and into the dark bedroom not being able to see in the almost dark because I had been out in the bright sunlight and my eyes were not adjusted yet. I swished to her bed. "Charlotte Ann," I exclaimed, "are you here?" and I thrust my hands down into her crib to see if she was.

Then I got the most terrible feeling I'd had in my life. I just felt terrible—*awful!* A million worried thoughts were whirling around in my mind, *for Charlotte Ann wasn't there. She was gone!*

Gone! Gone away somewhere and I didn't know where.

Just then I heard a heavy rumbling noise outside the house like a wagon makes going across the Sugar Creek bridge. It also sounded a little bit like a powerful automobile motor starting—but of course it couldn't be that because any car outside wouldn't be just starting; it would be stopping instead.

The second I knew Charlotte Ann wasn't in her crib I hurried out of the room, calling her name and looking in every other room in the house—upstairs and down—calling and looking frantically. She *had* to be in the house. *Had* to be!

But she wasn't. I came dashing back downstairs and out through the back screen door just as Mr.

Everhard got there. He didn't act as worried as I felt, but the fleeting glimpse I got of his face when I told him, "There's nobody here" didn't make me feel any better.

Just then I heard the rumbling noise again, only it was louder and closer. I looked up toward the sky and the sound had come from a big, black cloud in the southwest, over the tops of the pignut trees and I knew it was going to rain without having to look under the wooden step at our front door. It was going to rain a real soaker. I could tell by the way a lot of angry-looking clouds were churning around up there that there would be wind too—and that meant every window in the house and every door ought to be shut tight, but with Charlotte Ann on my mind I didn't have time to do it.

"Help me look for Charlotte Ann," I yelled back over my shoulder to Mr. Everhard as I darted out across the barnyard toward Old Red Addie's apartment house, calling Charlotte Ann's name and looking for a shock of pretty reddish-black curls and an aqua-colored sunsuit.

The word "aqua," which I knew meant "water" didn't help me feel any better and neither did the word "sunsuit" because the sun in the sky was already hidden by clouds, and the wind, which nearly always rushes ahead of a storm to let you know one is coming, was already making a wild noise in the leaves of the trees in the orchard and the woods.

Just then there was a banging sound on the west side of the house and Mom's big washtub, which she always keeps there on a wooden frame on the southwest corner to catch the rainwater, went bangety-plop-sizzle across the slanting cellar door and the boardwalk and out across the yard where it struck the plum tree, glanced off and went on, landing with a kerwham against the walnut tree.

Clouds of dust, whipped up by the wind, came from the direction of the pignut trees, which were being tossed around wildly, and I knew we were not only in for a real soaker, but a lot of dangerous wind. The whole sky was already all covered with clouds except the northeast corner, which is above Strawberry Hill and the cemetery.

Charlotte Ann wasn't in the barn and neither was Mr. Everhard's pretty wife.

My conscience was screaming at me for being such a careless babysitter as to leave a two-year-old baby girl alone in the house and also for not locking the doors when I did leave the house.

Being a boy who believes in God, and also knowing that "heaven helps them that help themselves" as Dad had told me, some of the stormy thoughts that were whirligigging in my mind were all mixed up with worried prayers and wondering what my parents would think with their baby lost in the storm.

Charlotte Ann, being a two-year-old and a "great imitator," having seen me go rushing out our back door and across the lawn, through the gate and past "Theodore Collins" on our mailbox, probably had done that thing herself. By this time she could be through the rail fence on the other side of the road and toddling along as fast as a two-year-old can toddle —getting up and falling down and getting up again— she was probably away down in the woods and maybe had already gotten to the spring and the creek—and you know what could have happened to her.

Just then the wind swept off my straw hat and sent it on a high, wild flight out across the yard, straight toward the walnut tree where it swished between the two ropes of the rope swing, went on and landed in the dusty road, was picked up again by the wind and whipped out toward the rail fence itself in the direction of Strawberry Hill and the old cemetery.

I was wishing my parents were there to help me. I was also glad they weren't there because it would be time soon enough for Mom to start worrying—and once Mom gets started worrying it's hard for her to stop unless she takes a minute to quick read or remember a Bible verse and then that verse is just like a new broom—it sweeps the worry clear out of her mind, she says.

The most important thing in the world right then was to find Charlotte Ann and not let her get caught in what I could tell was the beginning of a terrific storm. I was having a hard time to stay on my feet myself and I knew a wind like that would blow Charlotte Ann over as easy as anything. Of course, when a baby falls down it generally doesn't hurt much because a baby doesn't have as far to fall as a grownup person. But a wind like this one could not only blow her off her feet, but could slam her against a tree or a rail fence or into the briers of a rosebush, or if she was anywhere near the creek, it might actually blow her into it.

So, scared half to death, I yelled to Mr. Everhard, "Come on! We've got to find them!"

Say, that man snapped into the fastest life I had ever seen a dignified man snap into. Both of us right away were hurrying past "Theodore Collins" on our mailbox and soon we were out in the woods. "If they are anywhere near the tent or the station wagon, they will probably go there to get out of the rain," he said. "Let's go back to camp first." We were already on the way, before he finished gasping out the last word of what he had started to say.

We hoped that they were not in the tent, though, because the wind might blow the tent over. If they had gotten into the station wagon, it would be a lot better. Mr. Everhard was yelling that to me above the roar of the storm as we raced along, dodging around the trees and bushes and leaping over fallen logs. It seemed like we'd never get there. In fact, it seemed like it had never taken me so long in my whole life to get to that part of the woods. Then I felt a splatter of rain on my hand and another on my face and in a jiffy it was just like a whole skyful of water was falling and the rain was coming down the way it does when Mom says it's coming down in sheets. In fact, it started coming down so hard I couldn't see which way I was going. The rain in my face and eyes and on my bare red head kept me straining to see anything.

It must have taken us almost fifteen minutes—which seemed like an hour—to get to the tent, which I noticed was still standing—but not all of it. The wing which had had the green canvas roof and the netting sidewalls was all squashed in. A great big, dead branch from the oak tree under which the tent had been pitched—and shouldn't have been—had fallen on it, smashing the baby playpen and other things in that little room. The rest of the tent was only half standing.

For a minute, I imagined Charlotte Ann and Mrs. Everhard in there somewhere, the big branch having fallen on them. They might be terribly hurt or even worse. They might not even be alive.

Beside me I could hear Mr. Everhard saying something and it sounded like some kind of a prayer. I couldn't hear him very well, but I caught just enough of the words: "O dear God, please spare her life. Spare her and I'll be a better man. I'll do right. I'll—I'll give my heart to You and be a Christian."

Even as I stumbled blindly along with him the last few rods to the twisted-up tent, I couldn't help but think what I had heard our minister say lots of times, which was that even a kind man could still not be an honest-to-goodness Christian. Mr. Everhard might not even have given his heart to God yet nor had his sins forgiven, I thought.

I also couldn't help but think how swell it would be if Mr. and Mrs. Everhard would honest-to-goodness for sure give their hearts to God and be saved and confess it some Sunday morning in the Sugar Creek church like other people did almost every month.

Well, it took us about half a minute to get there in that blinding rainstorm and look inside the part of the tent that was still standing to find out that neither Charlotte Ann nor Frances Everhard was there. Say, as glad as I was that the dead tree branch hadn't fallen on them, I still didn't feel much relieved because I knew that they were somewhere else and if they weren't in the station wagon they were still out in the dangerous storm and nobody knew where. I also thought that if the dead branch of this old oak tree could break off in a storm like this, the branches of other trees could do the same thing—and if anybody happened to be under the tree at the time—

We both kept calling and yelling.

We made a dive outside the tent to the station wagon, but there wasn't anybody there and so we hurried back to the tent again, calling and yelling, trying to make ourselves heard above the roar of the wind and the rain and the thunder, which kept crashing all around us all the time. But we didn't hear any answer.

12

WHILE WE WERE STILL LOOKING into that part of the tent that was still standing, it seemed good not to have any rain beating down on my face and bare head. In a quick look around I noticed, even in the dim light, the interesting camp equipment such as a three-burner camp stove, a metal rollaway bed and a rollaway table, on which was a pad of writing paper with a flashlight lying beside it. Also on the table was a kerosene lantern which was probably the same one Mrs. Everhard had been using the night we had seen her digging in the old cemetery beside Sarah Paddler's tombstone. Hanging from one of the leaning tent poles was a religious calendar with a picture of the good Samaritan on it, showing the man who had gone down from Jerusalem to Jericho and had fallen among thieves who had robbed him and left him half dead. The man was getting his wounds bound up by the good Samaritan.

For just a second it seemed like I myself was trying to be a good Samaritan and couldn't be because the person I was trying to be a good Samaritan to was lost and I couldn't find her.

I hoped that when we *did* find Charlotte Ann and Mrs. Everhard they wouldn't be half dead like the man in the Bible story was.

I also noticed that some of the numbers of the calendar had circles around them which somebody had made with a red pencil or red ink. Without thinking, I said, "That's a pretty picture on that calendar."

Mr. Everhard must not have heard me because he looked all around and said above the roar of the storm, "The shovel's gone! She's gone out to dig again. Let's go find her, quick!"

As much as I wanted to help find Mrs. Everhard I was worrying worst about Charlotte Ann. So I said, "What about Charlotte Ann?"

"Look," he said, "she's left a note!" He picked up the pad of paper and shined the flashlight on his wife's handwriting and started in reading, with me looking over his elbow. I know it isn't polite to do it, but I did it anyway because the note might have had something in it about Charlotte Ann. This is what it said:

DEAREST,

I had another one of my spells and when I came to myself I was digging over near the rail fence across from the Collins house. I was still very depressed but when I looked up I saw dear little Charlotte Ann toddling out across the road all by herself. The minute I saw her all the clouds in my mind cleared away and I felt immediately happy. The little darling was all alone. I took her back across the road to the house but there was no one at home. I couldn't understand why they would go away and leave her all alone, but it was her nap time and I thought maybe Bill might have gone to camp to take us a jug of water, so I brought her back with me to camp. But you were still away so she and I have gone for a little stroll down along the creek. I think we will go across the north road today because I want to see if I can hear the wood thrush again down by the swamp. If we don't get back soon and you want to follow us, you will know where to look. I have mastered the wood thrush song at last so I will have a new whistle from now on. Besides the turtledove is a little mournful for one who is beginning to be happy.

All my love,
FRAN

It was a very nice letter for a woman to write to her husband, I thought, and when I finished I liked both of them better. In fact, for a jiffy I had a kind of homesick feeling in my heart like I wished there was somebody in the world, besides the gang and my parents, who liked me.

But I didn't have time to wish anything like that because an even worse worry startled me into some very fast action, for I remembered that the path on the other side of the north road, if you followed it far enough, not only led to the old swamp but went on through it. It is the path the gang always takes to go to Old Man Paddler's cabin in the hills, and about

113

twenty feet to the left of the path, as it goes through the swamp, is some quicksand. Maybe you remember the dark night when Little Tom Till's drunkard dad got lost in the swamp and sank down into the mire all the way up to his chin; and when our flashlights found him out there, all we could see was his scared face and head, and it looked like a man's head lying in the swamp.

"We've really got to hurry now," I said to Mr. Everhard and told him why. "They probably got to the swamp before the storm struck, but it's so dark down there in that part of the woods they couldn't see the path and maybe they will get out into the swamp. *Quick!*" I exclaimed. "Let's go!"

I didn't wait for him to decide to follow me, but swung around and flung open the flopping tent flap. The two of us dashed out into the storm.

To get to the swamp at the quickest possible moment was the first and most important thing in the world.

We stumbled our excited, rain-blinded way toward the Sugar Creek bridge where our path crossed the north road. I led the way, being careful to keep out in the open so we wouldn't run the risk of getting struck by falling trees or branches—also staying away from the tallest trees and especially the tall oak trees, which are the kind of trees lightning strikes more than any other kind.

I won't even take time to tell you about that wild,

worried race. All the way, though, I was hoping that we would get there in time to save Charlotte Ann and Mrs. Everhard from getting out into the swamp itself. I was remembering something Dad had taught me—and was also trying to teach Mom. "It's better for your mind to hope something bad *won't* happen than it is to worry about how terrible it would be if it *did*." So I kept one part of my mind saying to the other part, "Why don't you quit worrying and hope everything will be all right like I do?"

And do you know what? That crazy part of my mind just kept right on worrying anyway.

Over the north road fence, across the road, up the incline, around the end post of another fence and along the creek we ran. I didn't even notice the different kinds of bushes and wild flowers that bordered the path like I generally do, such as the purple vervain and skullcap and the red-flowered bee comb, which honeybees and butterflies and especially hummingbirds like so well—red being the favorite color of all the hummingbirds that live around Sugar Creek.

I wouldn't have even noticed the tall mullein stalks with their pretty little yellow, five-petaled flowers that grew along the path, if I hadn't run kerplop into one and fallen head over heels, getting my right big toe hurt at the same time.

I was trying to keep my eyes peeled for a little aqua-colored sunsuit, which would be sop-soaking wet, and I suppose Mr. Everhard was looking for some color or other of a dress or a pair of slacks his wife might be wearing.

After what seemed like a week, but couldn't have been a half hour, or even a quarter of one, we came to the old hollow sycamore tree, which is at the edge of the swamp, and where the gang had had so many exciting experiences which you maybe already know about, but there wasn't any sign of Charlotte Ann or Mrs. Everhard. We were still gasping and panting and calling in every direction, but there wasn't any answer.

Then I saw something that made me almost lose control of all my thoughts—the big oak tree which grew on the other side of the path from the old sycamore, not more than twenty feet distant, had a great big ugly whitish gash running from its roots all the way up to about twenty feet. The rest of the tree had broken off and fallen and its branches lay sprawled across the path to the entrance, right where anybody who might have been in the path at the time would have been struck and smashed into the ground.

That could mean only one thing: Charlotte Ann and Mrs. Everhard would be on the other side of the fallen tree in the swamp itself, or wandering around on this side somewhere, or else they were under the fallen tree.

"I hope they're *not* under the tree," I made myself think, and yelled for them some more, without getting any answer.

Right that second there was a lull in the storm, when there wasn't any thunder, and the drenching rain almost stopped, and I knew that if it was like some of the Sugar Creek storms, it might soon be over.

And then, right in the middle of my worry, I heard the most beautiful music I had ever heard in my life—a flutelike bird call that was so exactly like the song of a wood thrush—or a brown thrasher, as some folks call that sweet-singing bird—that I thought for sure it was one. A second later, when I heard it again, I knew it *wasn't* because a thrush wouldn't be very likely to sing its thrilling song in the middle of a summer storm.

I remembered quick what Mrs. Everhard had written to her husband on the note she had left on the rollaway table in the twisted-up tent. Mr. Everhard must have remembered it too, because he cupped his hands to his lips to protect them from the wind and the rain and whistled back a clear, beautiful quail call: "Bob-white! Bob-white! Poor Bob-white!" And right away there was a cheerful wood thrush answer, and it seemed like it was saying," "Lottle-lee. Lottle-lee. Charlotte Ann. Charlotte Ann." Boy, oh boy, it sounded so cheerful that all of a sudden my heart was as light as a feather because I was pretty sure if Mrs. Everhard felt happy enough to whistle, Charlotte Ann would be safe and all right.

Just that second also I heard another sound coming from Mr. Everhard beside me and it was something

I probably wasn't supposed to hear, but it seemed even prettier than a quail or a thrush—anyway it must have sounded fine to God. "Thank you, Lord, for sparing her! I'll try to keep my promise."

Say, I remembered that the Bible says that there is rejoicing in heaven over one sinner that repents, and it seemed like Mr. Everhard had just done that. That is how I knew his prayer, coming out of a rainstorm, would sound awful pretty to God and maybe to a whole flock of angels who had heard it. In fact, they might have been listening for it, hoping to hear it.

The thrush's song hadn't come from the direction of the swamp either, where the fallen oak tree was, but from the other side of the old sycamore tree in the direction of the Sugar Creek cave. Say, my heart leaped with the happiest joy I had felt in a long time when I realized that the song might have come from the cave itself, which, as you know, is a shortcut to Old Man Paddler's cabin in the hills. I was remembering that the first room is about twelve feet across, not quite as big as the sitting room at our house. I also remembered that Old Man Paddler keeps a little desk there and a bench and a few candles. The gang sometimes meets there when we are in that part of the woods. We had even stayed almost all night there once—both ends of the night anyway—the middle of it being interrupted by Poetry's homemade ghost, which scared the living daylights out of most of the gang.

I yelled to Mr. Everhard, saying, "Come on!

They're safe! Hurrah!" and I started on a fast, wet run toward the old sycamore tree, swerved around it and went on toward the mouth of the cave itself. Just as I got there, I noticed that the door, which as you know had been locked for a few weeks, was open, and what to my wondering eyes should appear but Mrs. Everhard wearing the swallowtail butterfly dress I had liked so well that other afternoon when she had borrowed Charlotte Ann. Charlotte Ann herself was standing in front of Mrs. Everhard with one of her chubby hands clasped in hers.

"Come on in out of the rain! Come on in!" Mrs. Everhard said cheerfully. "Mr. Paddler has invited us to come up through the cave to his cabin for a cup of sassafras tea."

13

Boy, oh boy, I tell you it was a wonderful feeling which started to gallop up and down my spine and all through me as we two drowned rats hurried to the cave and went inside where it was so quiet we could hardly hear the storm outside.

"We got here just before the storm broke," she said to her husband—and probably also to me.

I noticed that the rock-walled room was all lit up with five or six candles, and over in a corner sitting at the desk was Old Man Paddler himself, his long, white whiskers reaching almost down to his belt and his white hair as white as a summer afternoon cloud in the southwest sky.

I noticed also that there were several new, comfortable chairs like the kind people have in their houses. Over on the east wall, hanging from a wooden peg which was driven into a crack, was a beautiful wall motto which said, *"For we know that all things work together for good to them that love God."*

Say, I thought, *this* is why he has had the cave all closed up for the past few weeks. He had closed it for repairs like they do a store in town when they are redecorating it. It was really pretty swell.

"How do you like our reception room?" Mrs. Everhard asked her husband.

He stared at her.

Knowing he didn't understand what she meant, she said, "Today was my consultation day, you know. Mr. Paddler has been giving me lessons in faith, teaching me how to trust everything to God and—"

I noticed while she was talking that Charlotte Ann was hiding herself behind Mrs. Everhard's skirts like she does behind Mom's sometimes when she feels bashful.

Then Mr. Everhard asked a question. "You mean you have been coming here for *consultations?*"

"Sure, every other day for over a week. I had a hard time sneaking away sometimes, but I managed it— while you thought I was at the Collins' and once when you thought I was taking a nap, but I won't have to come anymore." Her voice suddenly broke and I could tell that some tears had gotten into it; and maybe not realizing that her husband's clothes were as wet as a soaked sponge and that she had on her pretty swallowtail butterfly dress, she made a dive for him, sobbing and saying, "Oh, John, darling! I see it now! I see it! God *is* good! God *does* love me and I *know* we will see our dear little Elsa again in heaven! I have learned to trust! There *is* rest in heaven like it says on Sarah Paddler's tombstone!"

It was a sight I maybe wasn't supposed to see and I noticed that Old Man Paddler himself got out a snow-white handkerchief and brushed away a couple of tears. Then he adjusted his thick-lensed glasses and looked down at the Bible on the desk in front of him.

"Just this afternoon," Mrs. Everhard said with her face buried against her husband's neck, "when I saw the clouds rolling and twisting and I knew there was going to be a bad storm, I was so afraid for little Charlotte Ann and I prayed and prayed as I ran, knowing if I could get here, I would be safe. When lightning struck that old tree out there and it came crashing down in the very place where we had been just a moment before, I realized that God Himself was looking after us. So I began to thank Him and without knowing I was going to do it I was thanking Him also for dying upon the cross for me that my sins might be forgiven and—and all of a sudden I began to be very happy inside. Oh, John!"

Mrs. Everhard stopped talking and just clung to her husband while they both stood with their arms around each other, with little Charlotte Ann standing below them not knowing what was going on at all. Then Charlotte Ann quick looked up at them and, like she does sometimes when Mom and Dad are standing like that, she kind of beat her little hands on Mrs. Everhard's knees and said up to them in her cute little baby voice, "I want to be up where the heads are."

Well, that is the beginning of the end of this story—one of the most wonderful things that ever happened around Sugar Creek.

After the storm was over and the clouds had cleared away and the friendly sun was shining again on a terribly wet world that had just had a good rainwater bath, we said good-bye to Old Man Paddler, not accepting his kind invitation to go through the cave to his cabin for a cup of sassafras tea, because I knew I had better get back home with Charlotte Ann before my parents got there so that when they did get there I would just be finishing my job of two hours of baby-sitting. I maybe ought to close the windows too, and if there was any rainwater on the floor anywhere I had better get it mopped up quick before Dad or Mom or both of them at the same time saw it and started mopping up on *me*.

We were all the way to the Sugar Creek bridge before Mr. Everhard stopped to say, "Where's the shovel you took with you when you left the tent?"

Mrs. Everhard laughed a very musical laugh and answered, "I gave it to Mr. Paddler. He needs a new one for his flower garden up in the hills. Besides, I don't think I'll ever need it again—will I, darling?" she said to Charlotte Ann whom she was carrying.

But Charlotte Ann didn't seem to understand what it was all about. "I'm hungry," she said.

Just that second there was a rippling bird voice from somewhere in the woods and it sounded like it was saying, "O lottle-lee. Lottle-lee." It was an honest-to-goodness wood thrush, which probably felt extra happy about something, now that the storm was over.

* * *

When we got to the green tent, Mrs. Everhard just stood looking at all the damage the storm had done, none of us saying anything for a minute, not even Charlotte Ann. I was sort of expecting her to make some kind of a woman's exclamation, and feel terribly bad. But instead she said quietly, "Well, that's that. It was God's storm, so we'll have to accept what it did to our property." And I thought what a wonderful teacher Old Man Paddler had been.

Then she seemed to forget that Charlotte Ann and I were there, because she said, "It's been a wonderful vacation, John, *wonderful*! I'll never be able to thank God enough for such a thoughtful husband, and for that dear old man in the cave."

Well, I can't take time now to tell you any more about what happened that day, except that I did get home with Charlotte Ann at just about the same time my folks drove up to our mailbox. Mom was so thankful that we were all right that she didn't say much about the rainwater on the kitchen floor, and my wet clothes. Besides, the Everhards were there with me, and it seems like Mom thinks I am a better boy when we have company than when we don't. Besides, Mr. Everhard was all wet too, and it might not seem right for a boy to get a scolding for something it was all right for a grownup person to do.

The Everhards couldn't stay in the tent that night, so Little Jim's mom kept them at their house, for they have one of the best spare rooms in all the Sugar Creek territory. Tomorrow the bobwhite and his wood thrush wife could move back into the tent again—after it had been dried out and pitched in a new and better location.

*   *   *

Big Jim himself picked out the best campsite in the woods for the Everhards, and with some of our dads helping a little, we moved the tent and all their equipment about fifty feet from the linden tree. Then we called a special meeting of the gang to talk over all the exciting things that had happened, especially to Charlotte Ann and the turtledove—who had turned into a wood thrush—and her bobwhite husband. We spent maybe an hour walking around through the woods to see how many trees had been blown down or uprooted, and some of our favorite trees had, which made us feel kind of sad, but it was good to be together even though we couldn't go in swimming. Sugar Creek's ordinarily nice, clear, friendly water was an angry-looking brown and was running almost as fast all along its course as it does all the time just in the riffles. Both ends of the bayou were so full they came together in the middle to make one big, long pond, and I thought about how sad the cute little barred pickerel must feel to have their playground all spoiled for them. It certainly wouldn't be much fun for them to have to look at everything through muddy water. Besides, who wants to have muddy water in his eyes all the time?

There wasn't very much we could do that was exciting enough for a gang of boys and we couldn't even lie down and roll in the grass—it was still so wet.

"We can all go home and help our folks—maybe offer to hoe potatoes or something," Poetry said with a heavy sigh.

Circus answered, "It's too wet to work the ground today—don't you know that?"

"Sure I know that," Poetry answered with a grin. "That's why I said it."

"What *can* we do?" Dragonfly asked in a discouraged, whining voice.

It was Little Tom Till who thought of something that sounded interesting. "Let's all go down to the cave and see the way Old Man Paddler has fixed it up."

"Yeah," Little Jim chimed in, "and let's all go through it up to his cabin and see if maybe he will offer to make us some sassafras tea."

From the old linden tree, where we were at the time, we rambled along toward the bridge following the shore above the creek, which certainly didn't look friendly today, even with the cheerful afternoon sun shining down on it. I wished it would hurry up and get back to normal because if there is anything in the world that gives a person a sad feeling, it is to have his favorite swimming hole spoiled by a heavy rain.

"Ho-hum," I sighed as I was climbing over the rail fence at the north road.

"Ho-hum, yourself," Poetry sighed back at me.

Only Little Jim seemed happy. He was standing on the flat surface of the top rail of the fence. "What you guys so sad for?"

"Sad?" I answered. "Who's sad?"

"Yeah, who is?" Big Jim said sadly.

"What are you grinning like a possum for?" Dragonfly asked Little Jim.

That little fellow scooted down the other side of the fence, saying over his shoulder as he ran across the gravel road, "Because next winter I get to go to the Everhards' new resort at Squaw Lake and go ice fishing. And I can take two of the gang along with me, whichever two of you want to go. They just bought a resort up there last week and are going to move there this fall." Little Jim had found out about it while the Everhards had been at his house. He was halfway up the fence on the other side of the road when he finished telling us about it.

Well, this has got to be the last part of this story because I have to get started as quick as I can on the next one—a long and happy and exciting story about how *all* the gang got to go to the Everhards' resort up in the wilds of the North for a few days' ice fishing— up where there were a lot of wild animals living all around in the forest. Talk about a different kind of fun, and also a different kind of adventure! Boy, oh boy!

I also have to tell you something else that happened that very afternoon when we got to the cave—what we found in an envelope tacked to the door.

"Hurry up," Little Jim called to us—and for some reason his cheerful voice made me begin to feel wonderful as all the rest of us swished across the road, up the embankment on the other side and started on a helter-skelter gallop toward the cave.

Moody Press, a ministry of the Moody Bible Institute, is designed for education, evangelization and edification. If we may assist you in knowing more about Christ and the Christian life, please write us without obligation to: Moody Press, c/o MLM, Chicago, Illinois 60610.